ETCHED IN STONE

SUSAN HAYES

ABOUT THE BOOK

Adina thought she bought a new statue for her collection. Fate sent her a soulmate instead.

Stone has been alive for centuries but he's never truly lived. Created by magic, he was duty bound to watch over the Drummond family and guard them with his life. Now, his last master is dead and there's no one left to protect. Instead of gaining his freedom, Stone finds himself locked in his granite form, a living mind trapped inside a statue. Lost in despair and on the verge of madness, the days blend together into one everlasting nightmare...until he begins to dream of *her*.

Adina Diggersby lives for her art. Sculpting stone is her passion, one that keeps her busy enough she rarely has time to mourn the one thing missing from her life, someone to share it with. The last thing she ever expected was for her newest purchase to come to life and inform her he was her new protector.

Adina won't rest until Stone is free of the spells that enslave him, but unraveling the dark magic that created him will come at a price. Are these two souls doomed to be forever alone, or is their love strong enough to be etched in stone?

FOREWORD

Imagine The Worlds of Magic, New Mexico... A series that brings together outstanding paranormal and science fiction authors to expand a town where witches, aliens, vampires, werewolves, goblins, sorceresses, pirates, time travelers, and paranormal live in harmony - when they aren't joining forces to defeat the bad guys. A magical town where being abnormal is the norm!

I'm S.E. Smith, the creator of Magic, New Mexico and I invite you to curl up with each book now and discover all the action, the magic, and the love that makes Magic, New Mexico the ultimate go-to series for Paranormal / Science Fiction Romance readers.

For all the stories, go to MagicNewMexico.com. Grab your copy today!

CHAPTER ONE

"No way! That's not possible. He's nearly pristine after all this time? Oh, wow. Look at the detail. Someone spent a lot of time making him look that good. Hello, handsome, you're going to be mine just as soon as I click—yes!" Adina Diggersby crowed in triumph as her bid appeared on the screen. She still had her fist in the air when someone else submitted another bid, trumping her offer by several hundred dollars.

"Shit. You can't have him, he's mine!" Her fingers flew over the keyboard as she entered in another bid, holding her finger over the "Bid" button as the seconds ticked down to the end of the online auction. The amount was at the topmost end of her budget. If she was outbid again, she'd lose, which meant her only chance of winning was to swoop in at the last second and hope her competitors didn't have time to react before bidding closed. The gargoyle she was trying to buy was a once-in-a-lifetime find, and she'd stumbled on it with only minutes to spare.

While Adina hadn't inherited much of her mother's clairvoyant talent, she had enough to know when Fate was presenting her with an opportunity.

With less than ten seconds to go, she submitted her final bid. "Please don't outbid me. Please don't outbid me. Please, oh please, he's perfect and I have the perfect spot for him out front and—Holy crap, I won!"

She sprang from her chair and did a victory dance around the converted barn she used as her studio. "He's mine, oh yeah! Who's got the online auction mojo today? I do!"

"And Mom wonders why you can't get a date. Are you dancing or should I call 9-1-1 and tell them you're having a seizure?" Her brother's voice interrupted her celebration.

"Hal! How many times have I asked you not to sneak up on me like that!" Adina stopped mid-bounce to glower at her brother, who was standing at the door to her studio, smirking.

He shrugged and stepped inside, closing the door behind him. "If I stopped sneaking up on you I'd never catch you doing whatever the hell you were just doing."

"I was dancing. In fact, that was my victory dance. I found an incredible piece up for auction, and I just scored the winning bid." She pointed to her laptop and did another happy bounce. Not even her brother's teasing could sour her current good mood.

Hal came over to her and set a leather-wrapped

bundle on her workbench. "I swear we're going to have to hold an intervention for you soon. What did you buy this time? Rocks from Europe? Stones from Antarctica? Oh, maybe you changed it up and got pebbles from Tibet?"

Adina had to crane her neck to look up at him now that he was so close. It was entirely unfair that they were both half-dwarf and yet Hal was a nice, normal human height while she stood an underwhelming five-feet-three inches. Why did she have to be the one to take after her father in looks while Hal took after their more-or-less human mother?

"I don't buy rocks, thank you very much. I buy raw material for me to sculpt into art. And no, this isn't for a future project. This is something special." She turned the laptop toward him and pointed to the picture of her new acquisition.

"Damn, that is an ugly statue. What is that, exactly, a gargoyle? Holy crap, you paid how much for that thing? Are you out of your mind?" Hal pointed to where her winning bid flashed on the screen with a reminder that she had twenty-four hours to contact the seller to arrange payment and shipping.

Adina shook her head. "He's not ugly, he's beautiful. Look at the detail, Hal. He looks like he could come to life at any moment. That statue is hundreds of years old and still looks like the sculptor only finished working on him a few days ago. And you don't get to judge me for my shopping habits unless you've suddenly gotten rid of the tons of scrap metal lying in heaps around your property. I know damned well that steel costs more than stone. "

"That's not scrap metal, that's raw material—damn it. I see what you did there." He raised his hands in surrender. "Fine. I take back what I said about your rock collection. I will also grudgingly concede that your newest find is a fine example of someone with great talent—who tragically misused said talent to create something hideous. That thing has wings, horns, fangs, and a face only its mother could love. Well, its mother and you, apparently. It's going to give me nightmares and it's not even here yet. Please tell me you're not putting it on display or I may stop visiting."

"If I'd known that's all it took to keep your ass off my porch, I'd have put a big, scary statue outside years ago," she retorted.

"Keep talking like that, and I'll take back my present and go." Hal dropped a hand to the leather bundle he'd brought with him.

"Present? You brought me a present? You really need to learn to lead with the important information and leave the insults until later in your visits." Adina eyed the bundle with curiosity.

"Yes, I brought you a present. The last time I was here I noticed some of your chisels were in rough shape." He nudged the bundle toward her and grinned.

She unrolled the leather and squealed as she saw what lay inside. A brand new set of chisels, the edges gleaming and each of them stamped with the mark of

Hal's forge. "I take back all the mean things I ever said about you. These are wonderful, thank you!"

"You're welcome. A craftsman is only as good as her tools, right?" he said, quoting one of their father's favorite phrases.

She ran a loving hand over the chisels. "I'll save these beauties for my next big project. I think it's going to be a centaur. I'm working on the sketches right now, and I've got a couple of blocks of marble that would work. I just need to see which one calls to me once I've got it planned out. I was considering a battle pose. If that's the direction I go, would you be interested in forging the sword? You and I have never done a project together, and I thought—"

Hal didn't wait for her to finish before he interrupted. "I'm in. You know me, any excuse to fire up the forge and make a big, badass blade, I'm there. When you've done the sketches, send a copy to me. I'll start thinking about a design. Mom always wanted us to work together on something. She'll be thrilled to hear about this."

Adina laughed and rolled her eyes. "Remember her idea that we share studio space and call it the Sword and Stone? Can you imagine how that would have gone?"

Hal looked around her studio and shook his head. "I can't imagine sharing space with you. Stone dust everywhere, tools piled up in random heaps, rocks all over the floor, and Nickleback playing night and day. I love you, sis, but that sounds a lot like my version of Hell."

"Says the man who has his forge blazing like the devil's fireplace even in the height of summer and leaves deadly weapons lying around where they can attack anyone foolish enough to visit you."

"Inanimate objects do not attack. That poor broadsword was hanging on the wall, minding its own business until you tripped and slammed into it. I liked that sword, and you threw it in the forge!"

"I did not trip. It attacked me. Melting it to slag was an act of self-defence. And don't pretend that you and Anneke weren't messing around with spells trying to make a flying sword. She fessed up last Christmas after drinking too much eggnog."

Hal groaned. "If you can't trust family to keep a secret, who can you trust?"

"Might I suggest that next time you pick someone with a higher alcohol tolerance? Our cousin might be a powerful spell-caster, but she's a liquor-lightweight."

"Duly noted, though I don't plan on trying that spell ever again. I'll leave spell-craft to the truly talented and stick to forging sharp, pointy objects. And on that note, I should get back to my forge. You've got an ugly mass of rock to pay for, and I've got a katana blade to etch."

"See you for dinner Sunday night?" Adina asked. It was a tradition their mother had started when Hal moved out of the house. Sunday nights the family came together to eat and catch up with each other's lives. Attendance wasn't mandatory, but both she and Hal had learned that it was far easier to go and share any news rather than let their mother find out on her own. Nadira Diggersby was a gifted seer and clairvoyant, which meant that there was no secret she couldn't uncover if she put her mind to it. It was a power Adina had been envious of when she was a child, but age and personal experience had shown her the downside to that kind of power. She had the occasional prophetic dream and a knack for recognizing opportunities, and she was quite content to leave the rest of her life shrouded in mystery. She'd learned the hard way that some things she was better off not knowing.

Hal patted his stomach. "You bet I'll be there. Dad's making smoked ribs this week."

"Then I'll see you in a few days. Thank you so much for the chisels. I love them."

They said their goodbyes in the relative coolness of the studio before opening the door to the outside. The summer heat hit hard, and she stood blinking like an owl caught in a spotlight as the brilliant New Mexico sun dazzled her eyes.

"Ugh. Big ball of fire trying to burn me. I'm going back inside. See you Sunday, Hal."

"Some desert dweller you are," Hal snorted with laughter as he headed toward his dusty pickup truck.

Adina closed the door on the outside world and scampered back to her laptop the second Hal was gone. She wanted to finalize the deal, arrange for transport, and then she was going to take a few hours to research everything she could about her new acquisition. Every piece she bought had a story to tell. They'd been a part of history, first as a part of the earth itself and later as a piece of carefully crafted artwork. She wanted to know where this statue had been and what it had witnessed in its long life. Something told her that this one was going to be special.

Stone hadn't known what would happen when the last member of the Drummond family line died. His masters had never told him. It had probably never occurred to them that the bloodline they held in such high regard could ever end, but it had. The legacy he'd been created to protect had dwindled and faded until nothing was left but a solitary old man who spent the last half of his life roaming the moldering halls of what had once been a glorious estate.

After centuries of service, would he finally be free? Or would the end of his duties mean the end of his life?

In the end, the answer was neither. He was still alive, but he was far from free.

Stone hadn't been in the room when the end came for his master. He'd been perched outside the old man's window, watching from the shadows as his master's breaths had slowed and finally stopped. Not that the old man knew he had an audience to the last act of his life. Nathaniel Drummond had no idea that Stone even existed, and he would likely never have believed Stone's story even if he had known. No one had known the truth about Stone in generations. He was at best a family legend, a tale handed down through the years about the gargoyle that watched over the family and kept them safe from harm.

Now, the family was gone while he was still alive. Alive wasn't the right word for his current state, though. He was still aware, but thinking was all he could do. The moment Drummond had died, Stone's body had grown cold and stiff. The transformation to stone had come unbidden, and he hadn't been able to stop it. He'd had just enough time to return to his pedestal in the courtyard and resume his traditional crouching stance before the change was complete and he found himself trapped. Madness had danced around the edges of his mind as he'd fought to free himself, but the magic he'd come to rely on didn't answer his summons. He was trapped. A soul captured inside a prison of stone. He lost track of the days, adrift in dark thoughts and despair.

Then, the dreams started.

He'd find himself in an unfamiliar place full of red rock and harsh sunlight. Mountains rose in the distance, jagged rises of land juxtaposed against an impossibly blue sky. There was always a woman waiting for him. She would run toward him with open arms and a smile, her chestnut hair gleaming in the diamond-bright sunshine. She comforted him, her voice soothing even though he couldn't understand what she was saying. She was his dream lover, and when she was with him, the darkness faded and he had hope that there was more to his future than an inevitable slide into madness.

By the time the men came for him, Stone was in a near-constant dream state. He barely noticed when they arrived with ropes and a hoist to wrest him from his pedestal and seal him into a dark crate. All he knew was that whatever his fate would be, it would unfold somewhere else. He clung to his dreams and the hope that he would someday see the sun again. He was tired of living in the shadows.

He didn't rouse from his dreams until his journey ended. His crate landed with a jolt.

THE PIERCING SOUND of nails being pried loose caught his attention first. Then the top of crate was torn open and light streamed in.

"Hello, handsome. Let's get you out of there."

Stone came alert in an instant. That voice. He knew that voice. In a matter of minutes, the rest crate had been taken apart around him and he could finally see again. He was indoors in some sort of large, open space. There were tools everywhere. Chisels, files, hammers, and other things he couldn't identify. A large slab of black marble took up most of the area he could see, and for the thousandth time since Drummond's death, he wished he could move. He wanted to see the face of the woman who'd spoken. He needed to know if it was *her*. The one from his dreams.

"You are incredible. Absolutely perfect," she spoke again, the words coming from somewhere to his left.

When her hand touched his outstretched wing, the simple contact sent a shock wave coursing through him. Dear God, how long had it been since he'd felt the touch of a woman? His entire focus was on her hand as she ran her fingers along the edge of his wing, following the sculpted line of stone to where it met his back.

"The photos they took didn't do you justice," she mused as she continued her exploration, running her hands over every part of him.

It wasn't long before Stone was ready to scream with frustration and longing. Every gentle touch of her hands made him yearn to be free of his magical prison. Every word she spoke made him more certain that this was the woman he'd been dreaming of. But how had he dreamed of someone he'd never met and how in Hell was he going to be able to let her know that he was more than a well-crafted statue?

When the woman finally moved into view, he knew instantly that it was her. She had the same brilliant green eyes and dark chestnut hair. Even her lovely smile was the same. There were a few small differences —a smudge of dust on her cheek that he'd never dreamed of, and her hair wasn't loose but tied back into an unruly ponytail. The details didn't matter, though. His nameless dream woman was real. He had to believe that meant there was hope for him yet.

She continued her hands-on inspection, her every

touch equal parts torture and pleasure. After so long it was a joy to have contact with anyone at all, but he wanted more, so much more.

"There's not a scratch on you. No moss, no weathering, no stress fractures. I can't even find a single chip anywhere. I had them bring you in here because I thought I'd need to do some restoration, but there's nothing to restore." She rose from her crouch and looked at him with amazement. "If I didn't know better, I'd swear you were enchanted to resist damage."

Her casual mention of magic sent Stone's thoughts whirling. What did she know of magic? In this day and age, most people thought it didn't exist.

Before he could even begin to make sense of the strangeness of it someone else entered the barn.

"I'm back, ma'am. I got the paperwork you need to sign. Once you've accepted delivery, I'll be on my way. Is that what was in that crate? Damn, he's as ugly as he is heavy." A tall, lanky man walked over to the woman and handed her an electronic device. He had to be the delivery driver who had managed to hit every pothole and rut in the road between New York and wherever the hell Stone was now.

"He's not ugly. At least, not to me. He's a work of art," she said as she took the device and signed her name in a small screen.

"Whatever you say, ma'am. My job's just to deliver stuff, not stand in judgment." He tipped his baseball cap to her as he took back his device and then vanished from Stone's view again.

"Have a safe journey home," the woman called out.

The sound of a door shutting told Stone they were alone again. As soon as the driver was gone, the woman bounced on her toes several times and beamed at Stone.

"You're all mine, now," she said.

With those words, Stone was free.

It was a brutal and sudden transition. One moment he was nothing but consciousness trapped in rock, and the next he was himself once more. He threw back his head to take in a lungful of air even before he'd truly grasped what had happened.

I'm free.

He rose to his feet, his wings and arms outstretched as he bellowed in triumph and joy. God, it felt good to stand again.

"Oh my God!" the woman yelled and took several stumbling steps backward.

Damn it. He'd scared her.

"I will not harm you," he said, still too dazed by his sudden transformation to manage anything more reassuring.

She didn't look convinced. In fact, she looked downright angry. Not the reaction he expected, but it was better than abject terror.

"What are you and what did you do with my statue?"

"I am the statue. I mean. I was. See? Horns, wings. It's me."

"Like hell you are. Statues don't just come to life, and last time I checked, there were no such things as gargoyles. We'd have heard of them by now if there were." She took another step backward.

Realizing he wasn't getting anywhere, Stone opted to try something new. "My name is Stone, and I'm not going to hurt you. Hell, I think you're my new owner, which means I couldn't harm you even if I wanted to." He reached out a hand to her. "Will you, at least, tell me your name?"

"Adina," she said, eyeing his clawed hand with distrust.

"You have no idea how happy I am to meet you, Adina. I've been trapped since my last master died."

"I swear, if this is Hal's idea of a joke, I'm going to stuff him into his own forge."

He felt a stab of jealousy at the mention of another man. "Who's Hal? And no, this isn't a joke."

"He's my brother and…damn it, no! I'm not doing this. I talk to my sculptures, but they're not supposed to talk back!" She took another step away from him and caught her heel on a chunk of discarded marble. She fell back with a cry, arms flailing in a desperate attempt to regain her balance.

Stone rushed toward her, but even his speed wasn't enough to reach her before she hit the floor with a thud that made his stomach twist. She didn't move when he crouched down beside her, and when he touched her face, all she managed was a flutter of her lashes and a faint moan.

As first meetings went, this was going to go down in history as one of his worst.

"I used to be better at this," he muttered to himself as he eased her into his arms and cradled her warm weight against his chest. A quick glance around what he now recognized as an artist's studio revealed a couch tucked away in a softly lit corner. Perfect. Adina could rest comfortably while he got his bearings. By the time she opened her eyes again, he needed to be thinking clearly and back in human form...if he could take that form again. He had no idea how the magic that bound him worked anymore. With the Drummond family dead, their rules should no longer bind him. If he could appear human, it should make the second round of introductions go at a little smoother.

At least, he hoped so.

CHAPTER TWO

Adina's head ached and she had a vague sense of unease. Nothing definitive, simply a feeling that something was off. She opened her eyes and found herself staring at the hayloft over her studio. Not a good sign considering she couldn't remember lying down for a nap. In fact, she couldn't recall lying down at all. She started backtracking to the last thing she could remember. She'd been working on a commission piece and heard a truck outside. It was a delivery. Her statue had finally arrived. She'd signed for it and —Holy shit!

She jerked upright and groaned as pain splintered through her head. Something had startled her and she'd managed to trip and fall over, thus proving once again that she was destined to play the role of comic sidekick, even in her own life.

"You should stay still. It will help with the headache."

The last fragments of her memory snapped into place. The statue. It had moved. And talked. She turned her head slowly, her heart pounding against her ribs. The wood from the crate was still there, but the statue was gone. Either she was going insane, or she was in trouble. Neither option made her feel any better about what she had to do next.

"Please tell me I'm hallucinating," she murmured to herself as she started looking around the studio for the source of the voice.

"You didn't hit your head hard enough to be hallucinating. You were woozy for a few minutes."

That voice again. Deep, with a hint of gravel and an accent she couldn't place. British or maybe Scottish, she couldn't tell. She finally spotted him standing a few feet behind her, and her heart started beating in triple time. She had to be imagining things. That was the only way to explain why there was a jaw-droppingly gorgeous man currently watching over her with a look of concern on his handsome face. It was a face she'd seen before, but only in her dreams.

"Who? What?" she stammered as she tried to ask several questions at once.

"My name is Stone. I'm sorry I scared you before. The transformation isn't usually that sudden," he said.

Transformation. Hell's bells. He was still trying to claim he was the statue she'd purchased. The one that was currently missing. Oh yeah, she was definitely losing her mind. Either that or he'd already lost his.

"You're trying to tell me that you were the statue but now you're human? You can just, transform? Poof?"

He smiled at her, his granite-grey eyes showing no hint of malice. She'd dreamed of that smile and those eyes so often she felt as if she knew him already, which was making this situation even weirder than it already was.

"I don't poof. But yes, I can transform. At least, I could until my last master died. Since then, I've been trapped. I'm not sure why I'm free, now, but I'm grateful to you for releasing me."

"I didn't do anything," she protested. Once again she looked from the empty spot where the statue had been to the tall, dark-haired man conversing with her and wondered what the hell she'd gotten herself into.

"You did something. I suspect it happened when you took ownership of me. I—I was created to be a guardian. My duty is to protect my master, or in this case, my mistress. You."

"I'm not your master. I mean, I bought the statue, but that doesn't mean I own *you*. You're a living being! That would be wrong."

"Wrong or not, it's true. I'm certain of it. There's a way I can prove it to you, but it would mean my shifting back to my other form. Are you ready for that?" he asked.

Adina thought about that for a second, then shook her head. "No. But you might as well do it anyway. It's the fastest way to prove your story. If you don't poof, I'll know you're lying."

He lifted one black brow at her. "Indeed. Though, as I pointed out before, I do not 'poof'. I'm a warrior, not a bloody fairy."

"We've not actually discussed what the hell you are, yet. I've never heard of anything like you."

"For lack of a better term, gargoyle works," he said with a shrug of his broad shoulders. "Ready?"

"As I'll ever be. You'd think that living here I'd be used to strange and unusual things, but apparently not." She sat up a little straighter and gingerly touched the goose-egg sized bump on the back of her head. At least, the headache was starting to fade.

"You can explain that statement to me in a moment. To be honest, I have no clue where I am."

"You're in—shit!" her sentence morphed into a yelp of surprise as she watched Stone transform. It wasn't so much a shapeshift as it was a complete change. One second he was a man, the next he was something else. Something huge, winged, and made of what looked like granite, but wasn't.

"Convinced?" Stone asked. His voice was deeper now, but the accent was the same.

"Uh huh." Adina rose from the couch on unsteady legs and walked over to the massive creature standing in her studio. "May I touch you?"

There was no missing the flash of heat that flared in his eyes at her question. "You may touch me as much as you wish."

Adina felt her cheeks heat as she reached out and brushed her fingers over Stone's forearm. It felt like granite beneath her fingertips but there was an underlying warmth that she'd never sensed in any rock she'd ever worked with before. "Which is your true form?"

"All of them. I prefer to be human, though. And after being trapped as a statue for months on end, I have no desire to return to that form anytime soon."

"I imagine not. You were aware all the time you were trapped?" The thought of him suffering that way chilled her blood.

"When I wasn't adrift in dreams, yes. I was aware. It was hellish. Not knowing if I would ever be free again. Wondering if this was all there would be until I slipped into permanent madness. The dreams were the only things that kept me sane."

"I can't imagine what that was like for you. What I *can* tell you is that you've wound up in the one place on the planet where you might be able to find a way to make sure that never happens again."

"And where is that?" he asked.

"A place called Magic. Magic, New Mexico. I guess you could think of it as a sanctuary of sorts. A safe place for, well, beings like us."

Stone frowned, an expression that made him seem even more intimidating. "What do you mean, like us?"

"I mean magic users. Vampires. Werewolves. Ghosts. Trolls. Dwarves, and a host of other things that go bump in the night. Everyone here is something other than your ordinary human being. Well, almost everyone. We're one big, strange, chaotic family."

"I had no idea such a place existed." Stone blinked and shook his head. "Truly?"

There was such yearning in his voice that Adina's heart ached for him. "Truly. You're home, Stone. Or you could be if you decide to stay."

"I have no other choice. Where you go, I go. If this is your home, then it shall be mine, as well." He lifted his free hand and pointed to a spot over his heart.

Adina looked closely and then gasped as she saw what he was pointing to. Her first name was carved into his body in an elegant script. Horror filled her as she brushed her fingers over each letter in turn. "Does it hurt?"

He glanced down at her hand on his chest and then covered it with his own. "No. Though you are the first master I've ever had, who thought to ask me that. Interesting. It's only your first name. That's new."

"Your masters sound like a bunch of jerks. How long did you serve them?" she asked.

"I was first conjured into existence during what you would call the Middle Ages. I don't know the precise date. Suffice it to say I have served the Drummond family for centuries."

"Centuries. So the paperwork I have on you is accurate. To a point, anyway. Would you like to read it? I researched where you came from, your family, your history. God, I have so many questions I'm not sure where to start."

"Perhaps we should start by getting you back to

your house so you can rest. I don't believe you have a concussion, but I know your head hurts."

"I'm fine," she said.

"You're not. I'm bound to you, remember? I wouldn't be much of a guardian if I didn't know when the one I am sworn to protect was in pain."

She rolled her eyes and tugged her hand out from beneath his. "And that cinches it. We're getting unbound as soon as possible. I do not need another overprotective man in my life. That position is filled twice over."

"I assume one of those men is your brother. Who is the other one?" Stone asked.

"My dad. Have you ever met a dwarven father before? What they lack in stature they make up for in stubbornness and a tendency to think of their daughters as treasures to be guarded at all costs. In my case, I got the added bonus of having both a father and a brother who forge sharp, pointy weapons for a living. And then my mother wonders why I don't date!"

"You're a dwarf?"

"Half dwarf. My mother's human, but she's a seer. Depending on her mood she'll either claim to be descended from the Oracle at Delphi or Cassandra of Troy." Adina grinned up at the bewildered beast staring at her in shock. "Welcome to Magic."

STONE LOOKED down at the short, curvy woman who

now ruled his life and tried to come to terms with all she'd told him. It was hard to believe what she said, but how else could he explain how easily she'd accepted the reality of who and what he was? Not even his own masters had always believed so quickly.

"I think I need a drink," he muttered.

"That sounds like a brilliant idea. And I guess that answers my question about whether you eat or drink," she said.

"I can, and I do, but I do not need it to survive. I used to enjoy eating, though. It's been a century or more since I've had that pleasure."

She gawked at him. "A century? In that case, you're coming with me right now and we're going to have a drink and something to eat. I'll try to answer your questions and you can try to answer mine."

"After you rest. Or at the very least take something for your discomfort," he reminded her.

"Okay, I'll take some ibuprofen when we get to the house." She paused and eyed him thoughtfully. "Not that you're going to fit in my house like that. Maybe you better switch to human form before we go."

"It would be my pleasure. It's been a long time since I've been permitted to use that form."

"Geeze. Your masters were something else. No eating, no drinking, no passing for human. Not caring how you were feeling or if you were in pain." Adina took a step back and crossed her arms over her chest. "As far as I'm concerned, you're free to do whatever you want. Eat, drink, use whatever form you like. If there are any other orders you need me to undo, let me know."

Stone opened his mouth to say something but words failed him. There was no way to express his gratitude for all she'd done. In the short time he'd known her, she'd treated him with more decency and compassion than he'd known in years. Instead of speaking he brushed his knuckles over her cheek, being careful to keep his talons away from her delicate skin. When she turned her head to nuzzle against his touch, it was all he could do not to pull her into his arms and hold her the way he had in his dreams.

He stroked her cheek once more and then shifted to his human form. When it was done, he found Adina looking at him intently with her head cocked to one side.

"Something wrong?" he asked.

"I'm wondering where you stash your clothes when you're rocking the gargoyle look. And where did you get the modern outfit? I thought you said you hadn't been in this form for ages."

He glanced down at the black jeans and simple white T-shirt he was wearing. "Honestly, I've no idea how it works, I only know that it does. If I concentrate I can alter the outfit I appear in, but if I don't the magic provides me with something suitable."

"I know a few werewolves who are going to be green with envy when they learn you can shapeshift without risking public nudity," she said.

"I'm still trying to wrap my head around the fact

you know werewolves. I'm starting to understand why my appearance didn't cause you more distress, though."

She gave him an odd look. "You surprised me, but I'm not distressed, no. Something tells me I can trust you. I can't explain it better than that, but I trust my instincts. Besides, my name is carved over your heart. I don't think you could hurt me even if you wanted to."

"You can trust me with your life, Adina. I would never do anything to endanger you or cause you pain."

Her answer was a rueful laugh as she pointed to the back of her head. "The bump on my head begs to differ with you."

Guilt sliced through his heart at the reminder that he'd startled her so badly she'd been hurt. "I am truly sorry about that. If there were some way I could take your pain away, I would. I was created to protect and defend, not to heal."

"And I was created with a double helping of the klutz gene. I was teasing you, Stone. It's not like you pushed me. You can ask my family when you meet them, I'm my own worst enemy."

"You want me to meet your family?" He asked, stunned.

"I think you should, yeah. I mean, until we figure out a way to free you from this spell you're more or less my bodyguard, right? I'm pretty sure they'll notice if I've suddenly grown a tall, dark, and occasionally horny shadow." Her green eyes went wide as saucers and a brilliant blush colored her cheeks. "Uh, I mean horned. Tall, dark, and *horned*."

God, she was lovely when she was flushed and flustered. He was tempted to confess that she'd been correct the first time just to prolong the effect, but he bit his tongue. The last thing he wanted was to upset his new mistress by telling her that now that he was human again he was feeling every need that had been left unfulfilled in more than a century. In his dreams, they may have been lovers, but this wasn't a dream anymore. Somehow, she'd become his reality.

"I would be honored to meet your family. Even your overprotective father. He might not approve of me, but as it happens, I'm immune to sharp, pointy weapons."

She laughed, her earlier embarrassment forgotten. "That's a definite advantage, but honestly, I don't think you have anything to worry about. Dad only breaks out the blades when he's meeting someone I'm dating. You're my bodyguard, not my boyfriend."

"It's a father's prerogative to test any man who comes courting his daughter. Anyone who was discouraged by a show of fatherly force doesn't deserve your affection."

"That's more or less what Dad said the last time it happened. He wasn't as eloquent as you were, but the point was the same."

"Were I courting a woman as lovely as you, Adina, I can tell you that I wouldn't let anything or anyone discourage me."

Adina blushed again. "That's sweet of you to say.

Come on, we should head inside and find that drink we were talking about."

"Are you feeling well enough to make the walk or shall I carry you?" Stone asked.

"Carry me? Uh, no, really. I'm fine to walk. It's not very far." Adina looked almost panicked at his suggestion.

"As you wish." He offered her his arm instead. "Shall we?"

Her panic abated as quickly as it came and she placed her hand on his arm with a shy smile. "I think that's the first time a man has ever offered me his arm this way. It's rather gallant."

"You mean old fashioned. I suspect I will need your help catching up on modern manners and etiquette. Seeing it on television or the internet is one thing, but living in the world...I haven't done that in a very long time."

"You're familiar with the internet? How'd you manage the keyboard with those big talons of yours?" she asked.

"Carefully," he joked.

"I bet. That would have been something to see, a gargoyle surfing the web and watching cat videos. Wait, where'd you even get access to a computer?"

He shrugged. "The household staff lived on the estate. While my master eschewed most technology, his employees didn't."

She was frowning as they reached the door. "So you

prowled this estate like a ghost? There but invisible to everyone?"

"Indeed. In fact, I'm the reason that my former home is thought to be haunted. Things being moved, floorboards creaking, the residents feeling as if they were being watched. All attributed to a ghost." He opened the door and blinked in the blazing New Mexico sun.

"I should have grabbed my sunglasses," Adina muttered as she raised a hand to her face to block the worst of the sun.

Her home was a weathered farmhouse nestled in the shade of several massive oak trees. Of more interest to Stone was the stretch of land between Adina's house and her studio. It had been carefully landscaped, with gravel pathways meandering through it. There was a multitude of plants and flowers he'd never seen before, all of them clearly hardy enough to thrive in the arid climate. Scattered throughout the space were statues and stone sculptures. They ranged in size and styles, some of them nearly hidden by the plants surrounding them while others stood out in the open.

"Was this to be my new home?" he asked, gesturing to the garden.

"Actually, I had a spot picked out for you in front so you could guard the homestead. Of course, that was when I thought you were a statue. Since you're something else entirely, you can have the guest bedroom. Maybe I'll have you pose for me in your other form and I'll make a replica to go out front."

The idea of posing for a statue of himself had Stone laughing long and hard. They made it through the garden and all the way to the back steps before he finally composed himself. It was more than her suggestion that had him in such a good mood. He was human again, alive and standing in the sunshine with a beautiful woman who accepted what he was without fear.

He reached for the door before she could, opening it and gesturing for her to proceed him through. Inside the air was cooler and the soft colors of the walls diffused the light that came through the windows. There was a trace of sweetness in the air accompanied by a hint of cinnamon.

Adina was darting around attempting to tidy up. "I'm sorry the place is such a mess. I made cinnamon toast this morning and hadn't gotten around to the dishes yet."

"I'm not concerned about the dishes. I am concerned about you. You need to be resting or at the very least taking something for that headache."

"Does wine cure headaches? I believe I promised you a drink."

"I'm sure it has some medicinal value," he said.

She opened a cupboard door, picked up two wine glasses, and then turned and pointed to a cupboard well out of her reach. "Can you please pick us out a nice bottle from the cabinet? I keep it out of reach so I'm not tempted to imbibe too often."

Inside the cupboard were several bottles of liquor

and a small but well-stocked wine rack. He chose a bottle of red and rejoined her in the middle of the kitchen. "Where to, now?"

"Living room. While you pour the wine, I'll get something for my headache out of the bathroom and then we can talk."

"Wine and conversation. You have no idea how good that sounds to me right now."

"Just wait. Later on, I'll order pizza. And hot wings. And maybe some garlic bread." She eyed him for a minute and laughed. "Given how big you are and how long it's been since you've eaten, maybe I should order one of everything on the menu."

"Food, drink, and the company of a beautiful woman. You're making all my dreams come true." Someday, hopefully soon, he'd tell her exactly how true that statement was. He still wasn't sure why she'd been in his dreams. He'd never dreamed of any of his other masters. Not until her. Adina was special, and he wanted her to know that dreaming of her was all that kept the darkness at bay while he was trapped.

She'd saved him twice now. Once from madness and once from his prison. Stone intended to spend the rest of his life keeping her safe in return.

CHAPTER THREE

MAXWELL WEBB HAD BEEN WAITING for this moment for years. In fact, his entire life and the lives of his family for generations had been dedicated to making this moment happen. As he stepped out of his car and onto the land that had once belonged to the Drummond family, Maxwell felt a weight fall from his shoulders. He'd done it. Everything that had been denied John Drummond's first born son was finally in his grasp. He'd gathered the important pieces one at a time as they'd been sold off to cover the Drummond family's ever-growing debts.

Cast aside because of rumors about Pearl's infidelity, Maxwell's ancestor had been raised in shame by poor relations of his mother. By the time the first Maxwell Webb had reached adulthood, he had committed himself to regaining what was rightfully his by any means necessary. It had taken over a century and been the driving force of every generation, but that goal was finally complete. The Drummond family was ruined, and all they had now belonged to Maxwell's descendant.

He didn't bother entering the house. What he wanted to see the most wasn't inside. He strode around to the back garden, careful to keep to the rocky path so as to avoid getting dirt on his handstitched Oxford leather shoes. Decades of meticulous research and recordkeeping had revealed every detail and habit about their enemy. Along with the hard facts and dirty secrets had come superstitious whispers of spirits that dwelled in the shadows, and of a guardian spirit who watched over the family. It had taken years to put all the pieces together, and even now, Maxwell had a difficult time believing the conclusion his grandfather had finally come to. The old man had been convinced that at some point in the Drummonds' past, they'd come into possession of something powerful, an old world relic that offered protection to whoever possessed it. Somewhere along the way, the family had lost their connection to the relic, and that was when they'd started their long fall into ruin.

Maxwell wouldn't have admitted it to anyone, but he was looking for a damned statue, a gargoyle as large as a man. His grandfather's research had led the old man to believe that this was the relic that had once powered the Drummond's fortune and power. Maxwell had a hard time believing any of it. Likely he was chasing an old man's delusions. Still, he'd made a promise to his grandfather, a deathbed vow, and he would fulfill it if he could.

According to his grandfather's notes, the statue he was looking for should be back in the courtyard area. Once he found it, he would claim ownership, and then whatever powers it had should come to him. If the damned thing had powers at all. If he wasn't about to make a fool of himself claiming dominion over a chunk of inanimate rock. He'd brought the family to ruin and claimed everything that should have been his ancestor's birthright. All that was left was this one promise. Once it was done, he'd be able to enjoy the fruits of his labors.

Twenty minutes later, Maxwell still hadn't found the statue he needed. In fact, he hadn't found many statues at all. Empty pedestals and holes in the overgrown greenery abounded, but someone had clearly taken everything else.

"Goddamn it!" he snarled and withdrew a phone from the pocket of his well-tailored slacks. He'd bought the house with the clear stipulation that he wanted everything left inside the house and on the grounds. Someone had screwed up, and when he found out who, he'd have their head. This wasn't over until he'd fulfilled his final promise and to do that, he needed the damned statue.

It appeared his victory celebration would have to wait a little while longer. He had a gargoyle to find.

～

THE LAST THING Adina could have imagined herself doing was spending the evening sharing a bottle of wine and a supreme, double cheese pizza with the man she'd been dreaming about for more than ten years. She hadn't dreamed of Stone often. Perhaps once or twice a year at most.

She'd never told anyone about her dreams. Her mother had always been a little disappointed that neither of her children had inherited her gifts to any great extent. If Adina had admitted to having a recurring dream about anything at all, her mom would have made a big deal out of it. If she'd ever learned that Adina dreamed about a handsome lover who came cloaked in shadow—God, she would have wanted to do a reading and find out everything there was to know about who he was and when he would appear in Adina's life. Adina had never wanted to know. She'd been afraid to find out he was only a dream, or worse, that he was real, but he wasn't destined to be hers.

She'd only come to her mother once to learn about her future. When she was fifteen, she'd wanted to know the name of her true love. An utterly cheesy question but one Adina had been determined to ask. The answer had nearly broken her heart. No girl wants to be told that her true love was not a person, but a calling. Not that she didn't love her studio or her life as a sculptor, she did, but rocks and stone would never love her back. Since then, Adina had never asked for another glimpse into her future. She didn't want to know.

"This was a feast fit for a king, and a goodly portion of his court," Stone said as he finished the last slice of pizza and leaned back on his side of the sofa.

"I'm going to need to eat nothing but salad for a week as penance, but it was totally worth it," she agreed.

Stone looked at her with a frown. "You will do no such thing. There's nothing to atone for, Adina. Why would you starve yourself?"

She blushed and instinctively tugged at her T-shirt, rearranging it so it didn't cling quite so tightly to her love handles. "I need to watch what I eat, or I'll gain weight. I'm half dwarf so I know I'll never be tall or thin, but I can be less, well, dwarfy."

"Dwarfy is not the word I'd used to describe you. I'm not even sure that's a word at all. Though the English language has changed so much over the years, I can't be certain."

"Is there a nice, old-fashioned term to describe someone built like me? Maybe we can start a trend."

"Aye, there is, *myn lykyng*. Thou art fairest of all things,"

Stone's accent thickened as he spoke and her pulse quickened as he complimented her. She wasn't sure what it all meant, but there was no denying how his words made her feel. Desired and beautiful.

"What was that first bit? *Myn lykyng*?" she asked, trying to reproduce the words in the same lilting tone he'd used.

He surprised her by sitting up, then taking her hand and lifting it to his lips to kiss her fingers before answering. "Roughly translated it would mean something like 'the one I delight in, or one who pleases me.' You are a beautiful and delightful woman, Adina. That is how I would describe you."

"You've clearly been out of circulation for too long if you think I'm beautiful. I liked the way it sounded when you said it, though." She tried to pull her hand out of his grip, but he tightened his fingers around hers, holding her fast.

"I know beauty when I see it, Adina. Whether you see it or not, I can," he told her, pressing their joined hands to his chest.

Adina didn't know what to say. Men who looked like Stone didn't give women like her a second glance. She had no illusions about her looks or her body. She wasn't beautiful, but her art could be. Her sculptures were everything she would never be, but in creating them, she added a little beauty to the world.

"You look like you're about to argue with me. Don't. You won't win," he told her.

"Are you always this sure of yourself?"

"Only when I know I'm right. Beauty is in the eye of the beholder, is it not? The delivery driver said I was ugly and you told him I wasn't, that to you I was a work of art. Your actions prove my point." his lips curved up into a smug smile as he finished speaking.

"You heard that?" she asked.

"I did. I could hear, and see, and feel everything you said and did even before I was freed."

"You felt—oh. Oh God, I groped you! I mean, I was inspecting the statue for damage but that was you and I —I think I owe you an apology," she said, barely aware of what she was babbling.

"You have nothing to apologize for. You couldn't have known I was alive and aware." His gray eyes darkened with desire. "If I were to be completely honest with you, I enjoyed having your hands on me."

At that moment, Stone appeared exactly as she remembered him from her dreams. Handsome, strong, and looking at her with such hunger that it made her body hum in anticipation of what could happen next. "Is that why you're still holding my hand?"

"I'm holding your hand because I want to. If you tell me to release you, I will, but I won't promise not to do it again. And before you even say it, no, this is not because I've been alone so long. This is something else."

Pulling away would be the smart thing to do. She should take back her hand, get off the couch, and start tidying up the remains of their dinner. Instead, she turned herself so that she was facing him, one leg tucked in front of her. "You're not the only one who has been alone a long time, Stone. I'm not going to ask you to let go of my hand, even though I probably should."

"You were never this unsure of yourself in my dreams," he muttered under his breath as he turned to face her, tugging at her hand so she was pulled in close.

"Dreams? What—"

He cut off her question with a kiss that left no doubt about his interest in her. His lips slanted over hers with an undeniable hunger that sent her pulse racing. Heat bloomed deep inside her, a firestorm of passion and need that grew wilder with every passing second. She let the flames take her. There was no point in resisting anymore. It was time to surrender to destiny. They were meant to be. Her dream lover hadn't only been a dream after all. Now she knew that she was determined to enjoy every minute they were given. For once, she wasn't going to let her mother's prediction overshadow everything. She may be destined to spend her life alone, but she didn't have to spend tonight that way.

Tonight, she had Stone.

STONE HADN'T MEANT to mention his dreams to Adina. Nor had he intended to kiss her, but somehow that's what had happened. He'd never been so out of control in his life. His first taste of freedom had him throwing caution aside. He wanted to revisit every pleasure he'd been denied for all this time and he wanted to experience everything with Adina by his side. He kissed her again and this time, she kissed him back. That was all the invitation he needed. Without breaking their kiss, he released her hand to reach for her, drawing her closer still. When she didn't resist, he simply gathered her into his arms and lifted her into his lap.

She stiffened when he picked her up and the moment she landed in his lap she tried to leave. "No. Please. I'm too heavy."

"Too heavy? Sweetling, you're not even close to being too heavy, and I'm a little insulted you'd think so. I'm a man, not a milksop."

She shook her head, lips pursed and her eyes shadowed with worry. "You should let me up."

"Not happening. At least not until you give me a better reason." He reached up to tuck an errant curl back behind her ear and followed it with a kiss to her cheek. He wanted to be doing so much more, but now wasn't the time to rush.

"Please?" was all she said.

"I'm a gargoyle, remember? Even if you were too heavy for a normal man, there's nothing normal about me. I could lift you over my head with one hand if I wanted to. Care for a demonstration?"

"No. I believe you. No need for a demonstration. You're sure I'm not too much? I mean, none of this is because I'm your master and you have to please me, right?"

"Protect you, yes. Please you? No. That's not what I was created for. In fact, I annoyed more than one master by doing things they didn't appreciate to keep them safe from harm. Anything I do to please you is done purely because I want to."

She uttered a soft sigh of relief. "Good to know. I want to hear about what you did to annoy your former masters, but first, I need to know what you meant when you talked about me being in your dreams."

"I was rather hoping you'd forgotten I'd mentioned that. You've had a rather strange and trying day. Are you sure you want me to add to it?"

"It's been an interesting day, yes. But it seems to be turning out rather well. At least, I think it is." She gifted him with a shy smile and he felt her relax back into his embrace.

"It's turning out better than I could have imagined. I like the real you far better than the dream version." He paused to kiss her forehead before continuing his explanation. "I started dreaming of you after my old master died and I was trapped in stone. Visions of you were all I had to keep the darkness at bay. I was on the edge of madness more than once. You kept me sane and helped me to hang on. When you walked into view today, I had hope again. Hope that I'd get to hold you like this in the real world and not only in my dreams."

She was silent for a moment, her lower lip tucked between her teeth as she considered what he'd told her. Then she said something surprising.

"I've been dreaming of you, too. Not recently, but you've been in my dreams for years. I recognized you the moment I saw your human face."

"What do you think it means? I may be a creature of magic, but I have little understanding of how it all works."

"What does it mean that we dreamed of each other? Until today, I didn't know if you were real or not. Now that I know you are, I know my dreams were prophetic. I get those sometimes because I have a trace of my mother's gift of sight. I don't know why you dreamed of me. Have you ever dreamed of a future master before now?" she asked.

"I haven't. In fact, I rarely dream at all. I do not sleep often. It's part of who and what I am. I wouldn't be much of a protector if I had to lapse into unconsciousness for hours at a time."

Adina made a soft, sympathetic sound and raised a hand to stroke his forehead. Her touch was gentle, but her fingers were strong and roughened by the work she did. Stone caught himself wondering what it would feel like to have her caress him in other, more sensitive places.

"You don't sleep? So, what do you do all night when everyone else goes to bed? Weren't you bored?"

"I kept watch. For years, I stayed up nights devouring every text and document I could get my hands on. I had so much to learn. Later I spent the time mastering different skills, learning new things, and managing the family's fortune." He remembered those days fondly. He had decided that his duty to protect the family didn't have to be purely physical. He'd taken on the duties of management and had brought the Drummond family stability and wealth that had lasted for generations.

"All those years working for those ungrateful bastards. I'm sorry you had to live that way, Stone. I swear we'll find a way to free you from all this."

"They weren't all bad masters. There was a time I was treated like family, or at least as a valued and trusted retainer. You must remember, sweetling, that I never knew anything else. I was conjured into existence with a rudimentary understanding of the world, but I had no childhood, no dreams to let go of, no understanding of what freedom could even feel like."

"You said you hadn't been in human form for more than a century and that you were nothing more than a ghost story to the people you served, so what happened? What changed that you lost all that?"

He settled her warm weight deeper into his lap and stole a soft kiss from her lips before answering. "In the late eighteen hundreds, not long after my master of the time immigrated to the United States, he took a young woman from the local gentry to be his second wife. John Drummond had always been a stubborn, prideful man, but after his marriage, he became distrustful and jealous as well. His wife was young, quite pretty, and held no real affection for her husband. She quickly grew bored of married life and over time, that boredom grew into resentment. She began acting quite scandalously."

"Did you and she…" Adina asked softly.

"No. Though she did try and flirt with me to the point even her husband took notice. When he did, he ordered me to stay away from her. When she continued to seek out my company, he blamed me and demanded I give up my human form and appear only as the gargoyle. He took over managing the finances and other concerns, convinced that he could do it as well as I could. That was when the Drummond family started their long decline."

"He punished you for his wife's behavior? That's hardly fair," Adina muttered, her expression turning stormy.

"His pride wouldn't allow him to consider that it was his choice in brides that might be at fault, or that he was failing to make his wife happy. It was easier to blame me. Even after her indiscretions grew so bold that he could no longer pretend she was true to him, he refused to forgive me or release me from his earlier orders. I think he might have, given time, but then I had to give him some unwelcome news. That was the end of any chance of forgiveness for me."

"What did you have to tell him that was so bad he never released you? What could possibly have been so terrible?"

"I was bound to protect the Drummond family line and no other. When John's first child was born, I knew that the boy was not a Drummond. He'd been fathered by another man." Stone didn't allow himself to dwell on what happened that dark day. There'd been no other choice, but he would forever regret what had come about because of his revelation.

"Oh man, he could not have been happy to hear *that*. But none of that was your fault. That was his wife's doing, not yours. I take it he never lifted the order and died knowing you'd never be human again?"

"My master was furious. The child was sent away to be raised in secret. Pearl spent the rest of her life confined to the house. She died giving birth to their third child, a little girl who died only a few days after her mother did. Years later John died without ever telling his son that I existed. One final act of revenge against the one he blamed for all his life's failings. "

"That bastard. He screwed you over royally because his wife was a hussy? What the hell kind of logic is that? He ruined his own family's future because of his stupid pride." She wrapped her arms around his neck and hugged him.

"Aye. He was the last member of the family to practice magic, too. Not that he was overly skilled at it. He couldn't do more than simple parlor tricks and a few basic incantations, and he didn't bother teaching even that much to his son. I suppose in some ways, the family was already in decline. He simply set the stage for the final act." Stone pressed a kiss to the soft skin of Adina's throat as she held and comforted him. It was the first time he could remember anyone holding him like this, and he never wanted it to end. If this were to be his future, then he would gladly take every second he was given.

"We'll find a way to free you. Then you can decide where you want to live and what you want to do with your life. It might be safer for you here in Magic. We have spells protecting the town and the residents. Visitors can't see the truth of this place, and we look out for each other," she said.

"I have no intention of leaving Magic unless you do, Adina." Maybe one day he'd want to travel and see the changes to the world, but it would be with Adina at his side. He already knew she was special. Whether he was freed from the spells that bound him or not, he had no intention of leaving her alone. He believed that she was his to protect, now and always.

CHAPTER FOUR

Adina couldn't remember having a better date. Not that what she and Stone were doing was a date, exactly. She'd started the evening with a vague plan to feed her new houseguest and get to know him better. Somehow that had evolved into being in his lap, kissing, talking, and laughing until she felt like they'd known each other forever instead of a few short hours. When she'd said as much, he'd nodded in agreement.

"I feel it too. Maybe that's the effect of the dreams. I feel like I already know you. I can remember what you smell like. What you taste like." He nuzzled her cheek and uttered a low groan. "Only everything is better now that it's real. I want to know everything about you, Adina. I want to replace every dream memory with the real thing."

"I'm still not entirely convinced this isn't a dream. If I wake up tomorrow and you're gone, I'm going to be deeply disappointed."

"I can think of a way to make sure that doesn't happen," he murmured.

"Hmm? What would that be?"

He lifted his head to stare into her eyes. "Let me love you tonight, and I promise that when you wake tomorrow morn, I'll still be there, holding you in my arms."

Her heart stuttered and her tongue tied itself in knots, leaving her speechless. All Adina could do was nod in agreement, but that was enough for Stone. He gathered her into his arms and stood, lifting her with ease.

"Where?" he asked in a voice gone low and gruff with need.

"My room is down the hall. Second door on the left," she told him, pointing him in the right direction. Thankfully she'd actually done some housework this week, so her surprise guest wasn't about to walk into a room full of unfolded laundry and chaos.

His long strides made the walk to her door in a matter of seconds and the moment they were inside, he kicked the door shut behind them. He turned on the light before setting her on her feet, and the moment she was down Adina reached past him to flick the lights off again.

"It's more romantic in the dark," she said, hoping he bought her explanation. There was enough moonlight shining through her window to provide illumination.

"As you wish." Stone tugged her back into his arms and kissed her. One broad hand splayed across her back to hold her close as he kissed her with a single-minded hunger that left her breathless.

She gave in to the need to touch him, letting her hands move over the hard planes of his chest and up to the powerful span of his shoulders. He was all muscle with a body any linebacker would envy. One day she would capture all this male beauty in stone, that way even after he was gone she'd have something to remember him by. When she pulled his shirt up to place her hands on bare skin, Stone lifted his head to grin at her.

"One second," he said, and then his shirt vanished. She could see that in his human form, her name was still visible over his heart, but now it looked like a tattoo instead of a carving or a scar.

"That really is a handy skill," she murmured.

"If only I could make it work on other people's clothing," he said and tweaked at the hem of her shirt. "How fond are you of this garment?"

"It's only a t-shirt, I have plenty—" The rest of what she was going say was lost in the sound of fabric tearing. She glanced down to see Stone's hands had shifted to talons, and he was using them to carefully shred her shirt. "You're like some sort of walking Swiss Army knife."

Stone's eyes glittered with amusement as he pulled the remnants of her top away and dropped them on the floor. "You have no idea."

"Not yet. But I'm hoping you're about to show me,' she said. It was easier to undress when she knew he couldn't see her, and she quickly took off her bra while Stone shifted his hands back to normal and unfastened her jeans. She helped him take them off, but when it came time to remove her underwear she hesitated. Not because she didn't want this, but because of her own self-consciousness.

"I want to see you, Adina. All of you," he said.

"And I want to see you. I already know which one of us is the beauty in this relationship. You are...you're perfect, Stone."

"And so are you." He dropped to his knees in front of her. He leaned in to nuzzle several light kisses to the soft mound of her stomach before hooking a finger into the cotton and lace briefs she wore. "I hope you aren't fond of these, either, because they're about to meet the same fate as your shirt."

"Not really," she whispered, her words barely making it through her suddenly narrowed throat.

"Good." He had them off of her less than a heartbeat later.

She dropped her hands to cover herself, but he caught her wrists in his hands and held on. "God, I thought you were beautiful in my dreams but this... you...you're stunning, Adina."

"You're only saying that because there's hardly any light in here," she argued.

Stone pressed one last kiss to her tummy before raising his gaze to hers. "Actually, I have very acute night-vision. I can see you perfectly, and I like what I see."

"Cheater!" she said, feeling her cheeks heat as a blush chased over her skin.

"Never. I will never cheat or leave you, Adina." He tapped a finger to his heart, right over her name. "I'm yours. And you are mine."

She opened her mouth to speak but whatever she'd intended to say came out as a gasp as he slipped a thick finger into her folds and began to gently stroke the swollen nub of her clitoris. She dropped her hands to his shoulders to keep herself steady against the onslaught of sensation his touch triggered. He worked the delicate pearl with one hand while the other stroked up her body to cup one breast. His caresses were a form a worship, his gaze rapt as he watched her respond. When her hands were shaking and her breath was coming in soft pants and gasps, he rose to his feet and she found herself being guided backward until she was pressed up against the bedroom door.

"The bed's the other way."

"I know, but right now it seems too far away," he said before leaning down to kiss her hotly. His tongue slipped past her lips to dance with hers and the world seemed to spin a little faster. Stone lifted her arms and drew them around his neck without breaking their kiss. His bare skin was hot where their skin touched and she belatedly realized that he was as naked as she was. The hard length of his erection was pressed to her stomach, clear evidence of his desire. He reached down to cup her ass in his hands, lifting her with surprising ease. When she was eye-to-eye with him, she daringly wrapped her legs around his waist so that his cock was tantalizingly close to her soaking wet pussy.

"You make me feel tiny when you hold me like this," she whispered against his lips. She tangled her fingers in his black hair, loving the way it felt wrapped around her hands. A rush of need hit her and she kissed him again, nipping at his lower lip as lust overruled every other thought in her head.

"You are so perfect and I need you so much. Tell me you're ready for me," He whispered against her mouth.

"Yes. And Stone, I'm on the pill, we don't need a condom," she whispered back and he uttered a low, shuddering groan and raised her higher in his arms.

"That's fortunate, as I have no idea how to use one."

The tip of his cock rubbed back and forth along her clit in the last, aching moments before they came together and then he was at her entrance, the thick head of his cock spreading her wide as he filled her. He kissed her, tongues dueling, mouths mated so that his next groan vibrated over her tongue and his breath was in her lungs. He held her easily, using his body to keep her pinned to the door as he buried himself to the hilt inside her.

Being with Stone was like nothing she'd experienced before. He was bigger and far stronger than any other man she'd known, but it was more than that. The bonds that had been forged in her dreams became real the moment he claimed her and something clicked deep in her heart. Swept away by feelings beyond her understanding, Adina kissed him hard, then flexed her inner walls around him, encouraging him to move. He did so, slowly at first but growing faster with each pump of his hips. When her orgasm began to build she found herself chanting his name in time to his thrusts, her soft words blending with his ragged breathing as he chased her up the scales of pleasure.

She tightened her legs around his waist and gasped as he started moving faster, his pace uneven and his eyes ablaze with primal need. She came first, riding his cock as she lost herself in a tempest of passion that carried her away into a place of pleasure. Stone kept going, his control breaking a little more with every thrust. Soon enough he was groaning her name, his head thrown back as he emptied himself inside of her with on final, shuddering pump of his hips.

She let her head fall to his shoulder, her fingers stroking the back of his neck as he rode out his orgasm and then went still.

"Better than any dream I've ever had," he murmured.

"For me, too. The next time I dream of you I'm going to wake up and reach for the real thing instead."

Stone chuckled. "Anytime, sweetling. I'm glad you're finally coming to accept the fact that I'll be there whenever you reach for me. I'm not going anywhere."

She raised her head to smile at him. "I'm starting to hope that's true. Acceptance might take a little longer."

"You take as long as you need. I'm immortal, remember?"

STONE CARRIED his beautiful lover to the bed, holding her with one arm while he threw back the covers. Once she was settled in the center of the matress, he crawled in beside her and pulled the blankets over them both. She snuggled up to him so tightly there was no space between their bodies, and he knew it wouldn't be long before he needed to be inside her again. Now his human side was dominant, his needs and desires were riding him hard. Food. Drink. Sex. He wanted to indulge in them all over and over again.

"If you don't sleep, won't you be bored lying her with me all night?" she asked.

"Never. Besides, I have no intention of letting you sleep yet. I want to watch you come apart in my arms a few more times, first."

"And then what? You'll watch me as I snore and drool in my sleep?"

Stone shook his head. "Then I will guard my lady as she slumbers. It's my duty, and my honor, to do so."

"Well, if you change your mind, there's a television in the living room and my computer is in my office, the room right across the hall. There have probably been a few hundred thousand cat gifs uploaded to the web since the last time you were online. You need to catch up."

He tweaked the tip of her nose between his fingertips. "I'd rather be here, with you. I've been alone so long that lying here with you will be far more satisfying than anything else I could be doing. Unless of course, it's making love to you. That is the most satisfying thing I have ever done."

"You're too good to be true, Stone."

"Hardly. I'm a magical construct with limited experience living in modern times. I'm going to need your help to adjust. I've been a spectator for so long I've forgotten what it's like to be part of the world."

"Well, it's nice to know there's something I can help you with. Maybe we can come up with a surname for you, too. You're going to need one, along with some proper identification and other documents. I know some folks who can help with that. You won't be the first new arrival to Magic who needed such things."

"An identity. Money. I am going to need help creating a life for myself. And I think you should choose a surname for me. My first master gave me the name of Stone. He was a practical man and I don't think he gave it much thought. I believe you can do better with my surname."

She flashed a wicked grin and chuckled. "What about McHottie? Or maybe Mr. Stone Studmuffin?"

He laughed at her suggestions. "I'm flattered, but do you really want to introduce me to your family as Stone Studmuffin?"

She winced. "Right. Good point. Dad would go for the swords the moment he heard your name."

Stone leaned in to kiss her before making his request. "I'd like it if you named me something related to you. Not your surname, but something with meaning for you. You're the first one to concern yourself with the details of my life, or even if I was comfortable or not. I'd like for my name to remind me of you."

"In that case, what do you think of Carver?" she asked. "What if you went by Stone Carver? That's my career, after all, and it's the reason we met."

The moment she said it, Stone knew it was the right name. "That's perfect. From this day forward, I'll be Stone Carver. Thank you."

"I think I should be thanking you. No one's trusted me to name so much as a puppy before, and now I've given you a last name. If you change your mind, I won't be offended. About any of this."

There it was again. Stone heard her offering him yet another chance to walk away and knew the time had come to make something clear to his little rescuer. "Stop that, Adina. I don't know what inconsiderate louts you've been dating or why they were stupid enough to walk out of your life, but I'm not like them. I don't need your permission to change my mind because that's not going to happen. I've been alive for centuries and I have never felt this kind of connection to anyone. I'm not going anywhere, remember? You don't have to believe that, yet. But don't keep trying to tell me it's alright to leave."

"My mother says it's a self-fulfilling prophecy. I don't expect guys to stay with me, so they don't. She's always after me to stop doing it, but she's the one who told me that's what would always happen."

He held her close and rolled over so that he was on

his back with her lying on top of him. He tangled his hands in the silken fall of her hair and gazed into her eyes. "Your mother told you no man would stay with you? What woman would say that to her own daughter?"

Adina shrugged. "One gifted with clairvoyance and a very persistent daughter who wanted to know the name of her true love. Mom always warned my brother and me that knowing the future was a double-edged blade. When I pushed, she told me that my true love would be the rocks and stones I sculpted. That's why I know you won't stay with me. You're not my true love. I don't have one."

He frowned at her. "I see several flaws in your logic, sweetling. First, you dreamed of me, and I dreamed of you. That wasn't random chance. We were brought together for a reason. Secondly, even if I am not your true love, I'm bound to you for the rest of your life. I'm your protector and that's all there is to it."

"But she's never wrong," Adina argued.

"Maybe she isn't, but I do know a few things about destiny and predicting the future. My masters were once a family of very powerful magicians, after all. I believe our futures can be changed. Sometimes it takes a tremendous amount of effort, sometimes it's the smallest choice that can alter our destiny. I also happen to know that even the most gifted seer can misinterpret what they see. That's one of the reasons why prophecies are so irritatingly vague."

"My mother is going to love you. She is always

complaining that no one understands the limitations of her gift."

"And yet you've accepted her prophecy that you will never find your true love without question?" he asked.

"I—But that's—it's not the same thing," she stammered.

"I'm not saying you're wrong. I'm only suggesting that you might want to open yourself up to other possibilities." He lifted his head and brushed a tender kiss to her lips.

"You're very smart, you know that? I'm starting to see why some of your masters found you irritating."

"I've had centuries to watch and learn a great many things about human nature. It's an advantage I'm quite happy to use when necessary."

Adina muttered something he couldn't quite make out about cocky older men as she slid down his body far enough to vanish beneath the blankets. Seconds later she was kissing her way across his chest, and Stone chose not to interrupt her with any further comments.

She teased him with light touches, feather-soft caresses and the delicate waft of her breath fanning across his skin. Stone had to fist his hands into the sheet beneath him to stop himself from taking control. His cock was as hard as his namesake and his need for her blazed hotter with every touch of her lips. When she traced her tongue around his nipple, he couldn't hold back his groan of pleasure, and when she did it again, he gripped the bedsheet hard enough he heard the fabric tear. *Damn.* He'd have to replace those…and the garments he'd torn off her earlier.

Adina's only reaction to the damage was to laugh softly and redouble her efforts. Soon she was kissing her way down his stomach, exploring every ridge of his abs with her lips and tongue. By the time she reached his navel, Stone was hanging onto the last, shredded tatters of his control. When her mouth reached the head of his cock, he nearly came on the spot. If being trapped in stone had been hell, then surely being here with Adina was as close as a creature like him might ever come to heaven.

She knelt between his legs and wrapped her fingers around the base of his shaft. Her calloused hands felt as good as he'd imagined. Better. He could feel every rough edge against the sensitive skin of his cock, a perfect contrast to the soft heat of her mouth as she took him deeper.

"God in heaven, you're going to break me if you keep that up."

A low hum of amusement was her only reply. The vibrations coursed through him, making his balls tighten and his cock twitch. She circled the crown of his cock with her tongue and his hips lifted off the bed in response. Every bob of her head and pump of her fist pushed him closer to his breaking point, and soon Stone found himself thrusting into her mouth with primal urgency.

That was the moment she released him and scrambled out from underneath the covers. Her hair was in disarray, her lips swollen, and her eyes were gleaming with laughter as she reappeared. "I think I have you at a *dis*advantage right now, old man."

"Witch!" he growled playfully before lunging after her. She was laughing as pinned her to the bed and covered her with his body.

"Nuh-uh. My cousin Anneke is the witch, not me. You'll meet her soon. She's the one I'm going to ask to help free you."

He bent his head down to kiss her as he settled himself into the cradle of her thighs. "I hope she can do it, but even if she is successful, I have no intention of leaving you, sweetling."

"I hope not, but I want the choice to be yours."

"Either way, I know where I belong, right here with you." He groaned the last syllable as he slid into her slick heat and buried himself to the hilt. Her inner walls pulsed around his cock and he knew that no matter what happened, this was where he'd always want to be.

CHAPTER FIVE

Adina had intended to call her cousin first thing the next morning and ask for her help, but somehow that didn't happen. Instead, she and Stone had spent a decadent day making love, talking, and introducing Stone to some of the wonders of the modern world he'd never had a chance to experience. She'd cooked some of her favorite foods for him to try, showed him her smartphone, and played video games. They'd watched movies, cuddled, and spent so much time in the shower they'd run out of hot water, twice.

The next day she contacted Anneke and asked her to come by in the afternoon. All she'd told her cousin was that she needed a favor undoing a powerful spell. She hadn't been ready to share Stone with the world, yet, and once Anneke knew about him, it would only be a matter of time before everyone in town heard the news. Anneke had many good qualities, but her natural enthusiasm and tendency to babble meant she found it almost impossible not to share happy news. Adina's vagueness had only bought her a few more hours, but that was time she'd been happy to have.

And any minute now, their hiatus from reality would be coming to an end.

"When did you say your cousin was arriving?" Stone asked, careful not to move from his pose.

They were in her studio, hiding from the heat of the day. A minor spell kept the temperature comfortable all year round without the need for heat or air conditioning, which made it a haven on hot summer days. She'd given Stone a tour, describing her current projects and what each piece would eventually be. When they'd reached the large piece of marble that would eventually be her centaur statue, she'd been struck with the idea to use Stone as her model. It also gave her an opportunity to get him to make his shirt vanish so she could enjoy looking at his gorgeous and well-muscled form. Stone was currently sitting on a stool while she sketched him from various angles.

"I'm not sure Anneke actually owns a watch, so the family has learned not to expect her at a certain time. It's best to remain vague. We tend to tell her to show up in the morning if we want her to arrive by the afternoon, and we tell her to come in the afternoon if we want her over for dinner. Since it'll be dinner time soon, I'd say she'll be here any time now."

Stone snorted with laughter. "The more I learn about your family, the more interesting they sound. Anything else I should be aware of before her arrival?"

She pondered that question for a minute. "You know the expression that some people march to their own drummer? Well, Anneke dances to her own personal orchestra. She's the kindest soul I've ever met and a very talented witch, but there are times I wonder if she lives in the same world as the rest of us."

He quirked a dark brow at her. "And this is the woman you're trusting to undo the spells that bind me?"

"When it comes to magic, she's exceptional. Her mother and my mother are sisters, and she got a unique version of the family talent. She can't see the future, she sees magic instead. We think it's because her father is part vampire and part witch. It's a potent combination, especially as she got his ability to cast spells, too."

Stone stared at her. "Vampires? There really are vampires?"

"I think I mentioned that the first day we met," she said with a smirk.

"Vampires. Next thing you'll be telling me there are mermaids in the town fountain…if this place even has a fountain."

"Don't be silly. Mermaids couldn't possibly live in a fountain, there's nowhere near enough space for them there."

"Wait, are you telling me there *are* mermaids?"

Before she could answer, Stone's head snapped up. "We have company. You can tell me about the mermaids another time."

"I don't hear anything. Are you sure?" she asked,

unable to hear anything that would indicate there was someone coming.

"I'm sure. A car. Small. Coming up the driveway." He paused. "They've stopped and a car door just slammed shut."

"That is impressive and a little bit freaky, Stone. I can't hear a thing."

"I have enhanced senses. I was created to be a glorified guard dog, remember?" He grinned at her and rose from the stool. He stretched, rolled his shoulders, and then held out his hand to her. "Shall we go meet your cousin? She's headed this way."

"You're not a dog, Stone. Don't put yourself down that way," she told him as she took his hand.

"I'll stop if you do, sweetling."

Warmth bloomed in her heart at his words and she looked up to find him staring down at her, his granite-gray eyes full of sincerity. "I'll try."

"Do. Or do not. There is no try."

"You did not just quote Yoda at me, did you?" she asked as they headed for the door.

"Movies were one of the ways I passed the time. At least, they were when I could get access to a computer or television. Star Wars was one of my favorites."

She laughed. "A centuries-old creature of magic who likes science-fiction. You're a conundrum, my friend."

The door to the studio flew open and Anneke launched herself through it with her usual breathless enthusiasm. Her blonde hair was streaked with turquoise and green highlights that clashed with the orange and yellow polka-dotted dress she was wearing and there was a crown of brightly colored wildflowers sitting askew atop her head. "Yoohoo! Adina? You in here? Of course you're in here, you're always here. Hey, hi! How are you—whoa! Who's the big guy?"

"Hi, Anneke. This is Stone, and he's why I called you. Stone, this is my cousin, Anneke Sokol." Adina did the introductions and then reached out to nudge her cousin, who was staring at Stone in amazement.

"What did you do, Adina? Wish one of your sculptures to life? Damn, he looks like he should be carved from marble and on display somewhere. That isn't what you did, is it? Because if that's it, then there's no way I'm putting him back. That would be a crime!"

Stone chuckled. "She didn't wish me into existence, no. But you're not far off with the rest of it."

"So what's the problem? A curse? I'm good with curses. Enchantments, too. I've been working on a line of love potions to sell online, but somehow I don't think that's why you called me." Anneke's eyes dropped to Stone and Adina's still-joined hands as she smiled knowingly.

"Stone's enchanted. We want to know if there's any way to break him free of the spell without harm," Adina explained while doing her best to ignore the blush heating her cheeks.

"Enchanted, huh? What kind of spell is it? What does it do? Are we talking something minor like random outbursts of song or something more serious? Which one of the locals did this to him, anyway?"

Stone tapped the mark on his chest. "I have been bound to a single family as their protector since the Middle Ages. The family line died out recently and I was sold. Adina bought me thinking I was something… else. Now I'm bound to her."

"Whoa. Seriously? Is that Adina's name on your chest? Damn! And after all this time and you're still hot as hell and look like you're in your late twenties. That's some serious spellcraft."

"My masters were powerful magic users at one time. I was created to serve them." Stone looked at Anneke. "Can you help me?"

Anneke's lips twisted into a wry expression. "I honestly don't know. But I'll try. You say you were created? Not summoned, but created from nothing, poof, tada, you're alive?"

"I don't remember coming into existence, but that is what my first master told me, yes. He conjured me. He had the statue created by a master artisan and then did something to it. I gather it took several rituals and a great deal of preparation."

"Hold up. What statue?" Anneke asked.

"Maybe it would be best if you showed her, Stone. It's faster than trying to explain all this," Adina interjected.

"I think you're right, sweetling." He released her hand and took a few steps away from her so that he was standing in the center of an empty space.

Anneke moved to Adina's side and gave her a wink. "Sweetling, huh? Lucky you."

"Actually, I think I'm the lucky one," Stone said. A second later the man he'd been was gone and in his place was the gargoyle.

"God, I'd forgotten how intimidating you look in that form."

Stone chuckled and grinned, flashing a hint of fang as he did so. His bat-like wings were partially unfurled, adding to his size, and the horns that rose from his brow made him appear a few inches taller. His face and body were that of a monster, but she knew that he was still her Stone. Man or monster, it no longer mattered to her.

"Holy fuck!" Anneke yelled.

"Yeah, I know. That was pretty much my reaction the first time I saw him, too. Only I didn't get any warning, first. One minute I was looking over my newest purchase, and the next I was face to face with a gargoyle."

"So this is it?" Anneke asked, taking a few steps closer to Stone.

"There is a third form, but I'd rather not assume it. I can turn to stone, but the last time I did so, I was trapped that way until Adina released me. I am in no hurry to take that form again."

"I bet not," Anneke murmured.

"What do you need me to do?" Stone asked.

"Stay right where you are for a minute. I'm going to take a closer look at the magic that was used. I think a little 'show me now' spell might help if you're okay with me casting it on you?"

"Do what you need," Stone told her.

Anneke uttered a few brief phrases under her breath and her blue eyes took on a glazed, unfocused look as she stared at Stone for a moment, then gasped. "What in the name of the Goddess did they do to you?"

Adina's blood turned to ice at her cousin's horrified tone. "What? Anneke? What did you see?"

The blonde shook her head, one hand covering her mouth. "I think the three of us need to sit down and have a talk. I can't—I'm not even sure where to begin."

Not once in her entire life had Adina seen Anneke at a loss for words. Whatever she'd seen, it wasn't good. Heartsick, Adina pointed to the couch where she'd woken up after her first meeting with Stone.

Stone nodded and changed back to his human form, fully dressed in black jeans and a gray t-shirt. His expression was as dark as his clothing, and the three of them crossed to the couch in silence.

What the hell had Anneke seen, and what did it mean to their hopes to free Stone?

STONE WAS USED to people looking at him with horror. He'd reacted the same way the first time he'd seen his reflection. This was something different. It wasn't his appearance that had Anneke distressed. It was something to do with the magic that bound him.

"What did you see?" he asked once they were all

sitting down, the women on the couch and him on the stool he'd been seated on before Anneke's arrival.

Anneke fidgeted with the charms dangling from her silver charm bracelet for a moment before answering. "You said that you were created. Conjured into existence. I'm sorry, Stone. That's not true."

Her words hit him like a sledgehammer, shattering the foundation of everything he'd ever known about himself. "Explain."

Her fingers continued to twist and toy with her bracelet as she spoke. "I'm sorry. Goddess, I don't even know how to explain this. I don't. What they did to you…"

Adina rose from the couch and joined him, standing at his back with her hands on his shoulders, offering her silent support. He reached up to cover one of her small hands with his own, grateful for her presence.

"Take a deep breath, Anneke. Whatever it is, Stone and I need to know."

Anneke let go of her bracelet and held her hands out in front of her, palms up. "You're not a conjured being, Stone. You're two things fused into one. Part of you is the statue you spoke of, a non-living construct. The other half is a *living* being." She brought her hands together and interlocked her fingers.

"That's not possible. I didn't exist before my master created me." Stone's heart thundered against his ribs and there was a low roaring sound in his ears. What she was saying didn't make any sense. He couldn't have had a life before this one.

Could he?

"I believe you did, Stone. In fact, I'm quite certain of it. Some of the spells I saw were related to memory. I think that whoever did this to you repressed your memory of who you'd been. Your first memories, can you tell me if you could speak? Did you understand what your master was saying to you?"

He thought about that then nodded. "I could. You're saying that wasn't part of the magic that created me?"

"I don't think so. It appears that your master stripped away all memory of who you were, but he managed to find a way to leave you with most of your knowledge. Language, muscle memory, everything a guardian would need and nothing else."

"That's horrific!" Adina said, her hands tightening on his shoulders.

"You're saying I was human once? That I had a life?" His free hand clenched into a fist as anger roiled deep in his chest.

"Yes. I've never seen a spell like this before. No one in Magic would ever use an enchantement this dark," Anneke said.

Shadows darkened Stone's heart as he heard Anneke's words. "So, you cannot help me. I will be as I am, forever. Do you think the people of this town will still welcome me when they learn I'm bound by dark magic?"

Adina leaned in so that her front was tight against his back and her mouth was close to his ear. "Of course they will. You're more than the spells that bind you, lover of mine. You're a good man."

"Until today, I'd have told you I wasn't a man at all. Now? Now I know that isn't true but I have no idea what kind of man I was. I don't even know my name!"

She threw her arm around his neck and hugged him. "It doesn't matter to me what kind of man you were. I care about the man you are now, and his name is Stone Carver."

Anneke cleared her throat. "I didn't say I couldn't help you. I said I'd never seen magic like this. I'm not the only spell caster in town, though. Not by a long shot. Give me time to talk to some of the others and do some research. I won't make you any promises, Stone. This won't be easy, but even if I can't undo everything that was done to you, I can try to unravel at least part of it."

"Whatever you can do, I would be grateful for," he said.

Anneke rose from the couch, her solemn demeanor melting away as she regained her feet. She flipped her brightly colored hair back over one shoulder and grinned at them both as if they'd all just shared a joke instead of discussing dark magic and even darker revelations. "I'll see what I can do. But I want your word that you won't give up hope, okay? And if you could please not mention to anyone that I can be all mature and serious when the need arises, I'd really appreciate it. I have a reputation to uphold, you know."

"You're secret is safe with us, cousin," Adina said, her words rife with barely restrained laughter.

"Indeed, it is," Stone added his own reassurance.

"Well then, I should get going. I have a lot of reading to do and I did tell Hal I'd be by after lunch. He's making me a new set of silver scythes to give to Mom for her birthday and he wanted my input on the final design."

"Scythes? Why would someone want silver scythes?" Stone asked, bewildered by the idea of a daughter buying her mother weaponry.

"What else is she going to use to harvest mistletoe and other herbs? I mean it's not like she can just go traipsing through the forest with a pair of garden sheers from Walmart. The dryads would be insulted!"

"The dryads? This place has dryads? I thought those were a myth!" Stone couldn't tell if she was joking or not. Surely she had to be, there were no such thing as dryads.

Anneke laughed and bounced off, waving as she went. "According to the experts, you're nothing but a myth yourself, mister gargoyle. I'm going to go and leave you two alone. Don't do anything I would do! No, wait. I meant don't do anything I *wouldn't* do. That's a much shorter list. Toodles you two!"

They walked Anneke to her car. Once she was out of sight, Adina turned and burrowed into his arms to give him a hug. "You must be feeling—I have no idea what you're feeling right now. What do you need from me, Stone? Pizza? A drink? Time alone?"

He wrapped her in his arms and held her tight. "I don't want to be alone. Later on, I'm going to need that drink. Maybe a great many drinks. For now, though, I need to clear my head."

"We could go for a walk. Or a drive. God, I haven't even taken you into town yet. You've been cooped up on my property since you got here." She went still and silent for a long moment. "I just realized. If you've been stuck in your gargoyle form all this time, you haven't been able to go anywhere, have you?"

"No, I haven't. By ordering me not to change forms, my master did his entire family a disservice. I could no longer accompany them when they left the estate. Sometimes I followed if it was night and there was little risk of being seen."

"In case what I said before wasn't enough, you're allowed to leave the property anytime you like," she said.

"Thank you. Right now, that's exactly what I want to do, but I want to take you with me. Do you think the neighbors would react badly if we went flying?" he asked, watching her face so he could enjoy her reaction.

"Fly? You can *fly*? Why is this only coming up now? As for the neighbors, who cares how they react. You're going to take me flying right now!" She was almost vibrating with eagerness as she bounced on her toes within the confines of his arms.

"I've been shot at from time to time, so it's a valid question. I won't take you with me if there's any risk of you being hurt."

"No one is going to shoot at you or call in a UFO sighting to the sheriff. This is Magic, not New York. The weird and unusual everywhere else is just a normal day here," she said with a soft laugh.

"I'm still getting used to that concept, though your cousin was a good reminder. She's very unusual."

"She is. I'm sorry that the first time you met her, she had to give you bad news. I know she seems quirky, but she's very gifted. I believe she'll be able to find a way to undo what was done to you."

He nodded. "I do, too. Speaking of Anneke, she's on her way to your brother's place right now, is she not? Perhaps you should call your parents and let them know about me before they hear about it from Hal."

"Shit! You're right. If I don't, I'll never hear the end of it." She popped up onto her toes to press a kiss to his cheek. "Phone first. Then flying. Then drinks and ice cream. Oh, even better. I'll make boozy milkshakes. You haven't lived until you've tried one of my mudslides."

"That sounds good to me." The darkness that had filled his heart since Anneke's visit faded in the glow of Adina's kindness. She hadn't flinched when he'd transformed today, and when she'd learned that he was an abomination with no memory of his former life, she'd gone to him instead of turning her back. She was a better person than many he'd met in his long life and he was beyond grateful that out of all the souls who could have become his next master, the universe had sent him to this place, and to her.

"Uh, Stone? In order for me to call my parents, I

need the use of my hands. You're going to need to let go of me for a few minutes."

He grudgingly released her and pointed toward the house. "I happen to like having you in my arms. I hope the conversation with your mother doesn't take long so I can get you back where you belong. While you're talking, you might want to find a light jacket. Sundown is coming and the air gets cold up where we're going."

She beamed. "I cannot believe you're taking me flying. I swear this will be the shortest call I've ever made to my parents."

Twenty minutes later Adina raced out of her back door. She'd changed into a pair of jeans and had donned a hooded, zip-up jacket. "Do you want the good news or the bad news first?" she asked as she came to a skidding stop at his side.

"Bad news first, please. Though it can't be too bad since you're still smiling."

"We're expected at my parents for dinner tomorrow night. Sunday night dinner is a family tradition, and I was told in no uncertain terms that I was coming and bringing you with me," she said, rolling her eyes.

"That's the bad news? I'd be honored to meet your family, sweetling. So, what's the good news?"

"Dad promised not to try and run you through with anything sharp and pointy. Mom actually made him hold up his hand and vow to behave."

"I'm not afraid of your father or anything he might try and do to me. I'm a big, scary gargoyle, remember?"

She laughed. "You're a sexy badass, but he's my

dad. He's going to glower and grump at you on principle."

"As he should. I suppose we shouldn't mention the fact that we're sharing a bed?" he asked, deliberately teasing her.

Adina spluttered and turned beet red. "Hell, no! That would be suicidal, and way more information than my parents ever need to know."

"I would never reveal such a personal detail about you, but I couldn't resist seeing your reaction. I swear tomorrow night I shall be on my best behavior."

"Be nice, old man," she grumbled and then glanced up at the darkening sky. "Can we go now?"

"We can as soon as I change forms. One moment."

He shifted quickly and gathered her into his arms the moment it was done. "Ready?"

"Oh, yeah." She was grinning as she snuggled in tight against his chest and pointed to the sky overhead. "Let's go!"

He stretched out his wings and leaped into the air. With a few beats of his wings, they were higher than the barn roof. He continued his ascent until they had a perfect view of the sunset and then began flying toward it.

"It looks like the sky has caught fire. It's beautiful," Adina said as she stared at the display laid out before them.

The clouds were painted in fiery hues of gold and red, and the sky beyond was slowly deepening to a glorious indigo. The mountains were an inky black that contrasted with the glowing color behind them. It was breathtaking, and yet he found himself staring at Adina instead. While she watched the sunset, he watched her.

She was lovelier than anything else in creation, and she was going to be his. She had to be because now that he'd met her, Stone didn't know how he'd live without her light in his life.

CHAPTER SIX

"Oh God, they're waiting for us on the porch," Adina groaned as she pulled into her parents' driveway.

"Is that a good sign? Or should I be worried?" Stone asked, looking unconcerned.

"Considering I usually have to let myself in, I'd say it's a sign they're anxious to meet you. God knows what Anneke's told them by now. I've been ignoring Mom's calls all day."

Stone chuckled. "Is that why you put your cell phone in the kitchen drawer?"

"Yes. I should have shut it off, but somehow it felt better locking the damned thing away after the fourth time she called."

"I can understand their curiosity. Don't fret, sweetling. This is going to be fine."

"How can you be so calm about this? What if they don't like you?"

He grinned at her. "Then I'll sprout wings, horns,

and fangs and fly you out of there. I'm bound to protect you from anyone and anything, including overprotective parents."

"I'll remember that. If things get to be too much I'll expect you to whisk me out of there," she said and shut off the engine. Before she could do more than undo her seatbelt, Stone was out of the car and heading around to her. It took her a moment to realize what he was doing. He was actually coming around to open her door for her.

There was something to be said for his old-fashioned ways.

He took her hand, helped her out of her seat, and kept hold of her as they walked up to the house. Her mother had already risen from the porch swing to meet them, and both her father and brother were standing right behind Nadira, arms folded over their chests and identical scowls on their faces. They were both wearing clean shirts, and Dad had even trimmed his beard. Adina looked intently at her mother and noticed she'd put on a few touches of makeup and done her hair. Something odd was going on. Dad only trimmed his red and silver beard for special occasions like holidays…and funerals.

Her mom came down the stairs to greet them, her face wreathed in smiles. "Hello, ladybug. Good to see you. This must be Stone," Her mother's smile grew even wider as she looked at Stone, confirming Adina's suspicions. The only time mom looked that happy was when she knew something she shouldn't.

What the hell was going on?

"Ladybug?" Stone murmured under his breath.

"Behave," she whispered back and then stepped forward to make introductions. "Hi, Mom. Yes, this is Stone Carver. Stone, these are my parents, Nadira and Joram Diggersby, and the big lug in the back who is trying his best to look intimidating is my big brother, Hal."

"It's an honor to meet you all. Thank you for inviting me into your home," Stone said and then released her hand to walk up to her mother. He presented her with the bouquet of flowers he'd requested they pick up on the way over and Adina swore her mom's face lit up like she was a kid at Christmas.

"Why, thank you, Stone."

Without missing a beat, Stone turned to her dad and offered him his hand. "Sir. Adina has told me about the work you do. I'd be very interested in seeing your forge someday if you would be willing to give me a tour."

"I'd be happy to," her father seemed surprised by the words coming out of his mouth as he shook Stone's hand.

Hal was still staring at Stone. "You don't look anything like the pictures I saw of the statue my sister bought. That thing was nightmare-inducing levels of ugly. How do I know you're really who, and what, you say you are?"

Stone met Hal's stare. "Thank you. My other form was created to be intimidating. It's nice to know it is still effective. As for your question, I don't have to prove myself to you. Adina knows the truth. Are you calling your own sister a liar?"

Silence fell, and Adina briefly wondered if it was too soon to ask Stone to fly her out of there.

Hal glowered for a few more seconds before finally smirking and offering Stone his hand. "Nicely played."

Stone grinned and shook Hal's hand. "That wasn't a ploy. If you'd called my Adina a liar, I'd have taken you apart."

"Your Adina?" Hal asked

"Mine," Stone repeated and walked back to her, draping a possessive arm around her shoulders.

Oh yeah, this is going well.

"I can see we're going to have a lot to talk about over dinner. Come on inside. I made lemonade, would you like a glass? Stone, I want to hear all about how you came to be here in Magic, and I know Joram is going to want to talk to you about historical weapons. Anneke mentioned you're old enough to have seen some interesting things," Adina's mother kept up a steady chatter as she herded all of them into the house.

"I was created—I mean, I remember the Middle Ages and I've handled a great many weapons in my time. I'd be happy to talk about what I recall, Mr. Diggersby."

"Wait, you *remember* the Middle Ages? I want to hear this, too," Hal chimed in.

The men headed for the living room while Adina found herself being shooed in the opposite direction.

"Come help me with the lemonade, ladybug," was all her mother said, but Adina heard the command underlying the simple request. Her mother wanted a word with her. Alone.

The moment they were out of earshot Nadira fanned her face and grinned. "That is one hot hunk of manhood you've got there."

"Mom! He's not a hunk of anything and where did you even hear that expression?"

"Stone is a total hottie. Charming, too. None of those other boys you brought over ever thought to bring me flowers. And the way he stood up to your brother—that was delicious. Hal had that one coming. I told him to be on his best behavior."

"I'm starting to think that is the best Hal can do. You tried your best, but he's doomed by his grumpy dwarf DNA."

Nadira sighed. "I think you're right. Of course, if you rat me out to your Dad, I'll deny ever saying such a thing. Now, how are you coping with all this? You went online auction shopping and instead of a new statue, they shipped you your soulmate. I imagine that's got to be a little unsettling."

"I—what?" Adina blinked at her mother as her entire train of thought derailed and then exploded for good measure.

Her mother frowned. "Stone. He's your soulmate. You've been waiting for him to arrive since you were fifteen years old, ladybug. Don't tell me you didn't realize who he was?"

"I don't have a soulmate."

"Nonsense. I told you about him right here in this kitchen. Don't you remember?"

"I remember you telling me that I wouldn't have a true love. Why do you think I stopped dating, mom? There wasn't any point when my mother, the seer who was never wrong, told me that my true love would be my stone sculptures." Adina shot past her mother and started pulling glasses off the shelf for the lemonade. She didn't want to have this conversation again, and she certainly didn't want to have it now.

"Oh no," Nadira murmured in the saddest tone Adina had ever heard from her.

"What, mom? Did you forget your own prophecy?" Adina asked without looking away from her self-appointed task.

"No, sweetheart. I remember it fine. You're the one who doesn't recall it correctly. I'm so sorry. I didn't realize. You never said anything. Is this why you've never come to me for another reading? Why you've ignored every vision and dream you've ever had? Did I do this?"

"You didn't do anything but tell me the truth. It was my own fault for asking. You always warned Hal and me that knowing the future wasn't always a good thing."

"Adina, stop what you're doing and look at me. I know you're hurting, but you need to listen to me." Her mom set her hand down on Adina's shoulder and coaxed her to turn around.

She turned and faced her mother as a storm of emotions she didn't want to deal with bubbled deep in her heart. "I'm listening."

"I didn't tell you that your true love would be your sculptures. I told you your true love's name was Stone. It was so obvious to me that I never considered that you might misunderstand what I was saying. I'm sorry, ladybug. I hurt you and I never even realized."

"You said—but that—-Stone?" Adina's words were as fragmented as her thoughts.

"Stone." Her mom repeated with a tiny smile. "He's the one fate chose for you. Or did you think you dreamed of him for no reason?"

"You went snooping into my future, didn't you? I thought we agreed you weren't going to do that without my permission."

"I snooped because my little girl met her soulmate and didn't even call to tell me. I knew something wasn't right, but I had no idea... You do forgive me, don't you?"

Dazed, Adina gave her mom a fierce hug and tried to fight back the tears of joy that stung her eyes. "Of course, I forgive you. It's not like you deliberately misled me. I'm going to double check everything you say from now on in case I didn't understand it the first time, but I love you anyway."

Her mom hugged her back so hard it was nearly impossible to breathe. "I love you, too. Now, dry your eyes, and we'll get these drinks to the boys. If anyone asks about your eyes, just say you got a bit of fresh lemon juice in them."

"Can you do me a favor? After the bombshell you just dropped, could you add a little vodka to my drink? I think I've earned it."

Her mom laughed. "I think that's a grand idea. I'll join you. Don't tell your father."

"My lips are sealed. Speaking of Dad, does he know about Stone?"

"He does. I told him as soon as Anneke called."

"Ah, so that's why he's behaving himself," Adina muttered.

"It is. As you might have guessed, I didn't tell your brother. He's not going to take it well."

Adina scoffed. "He won't care that much."

"Oh, I think he will. He came to me a few years ago and asked about his soulmate, too. I told him he'd find his after you found yours."

Adina nearly dropped the tray loaded with drinks. "Really? So his doom is nigh? God, I can't wait to tell him. Do you think he'll panic and go into hiding?"

"There's no hiding from destiny, ladybug. You should know that by now. Come on, let's go check on our men. If we leave them alone much longer, they'll sneak off to the forge and we'll never get them back in time for dinner."

Our men.

Adina let that phrase roll around her head as she followed her mother out of the kitchen. She liked it almost as much as the other words that danced through her thoughts. Soulmate. True love. Destiny.

Her destiny was waiting for her in the other room and she couldn't wait to get back to him.

ADINA RETURNED from the kitchen glowing with happiness and full of life. Stone didn't know what had happened in the brief time that she'd been gone, but whatever it was, it looked good on her. He'd tried to get her alone long enough to ask what had happened, but her family was never out of earshot long enough.

He knew the meal was excellent, but if someone had asked him what he'd eaten he wouldn't have been able to say. The same went for the conversations they had while they dined. He took part, answering questions and talking about his past, but he couldn't recall anything he'd said. All his attention was focused on Adina.

Finally, they said their goodnights and departed the same time as Hal, his big truck rumbling to life before Stone had even closed Adina's car door. He took his seat and immediately leaned in to steal a kiss.

"I swear your parents were keeping us apart on purpose," he grumbled.

"And they enjoyed every minute of it," she agreed and kissed him back.

"You seemed to be enjoying yourself, too. Did your mother say something to you to put that smile on your face? I noticed you were much happier when you brought out the lemonade. Or was that because of the vodka you snuck into your glass?"

"I didn't sneak anything. Mom poured the booze, not me," she said as she started the car and began the short drive back home.

"Celebrating or commiserating?"

"Celebrating. And how did you know?"

"You left your glass beside mine and I picked up the wrong one. Your lemonade packed more of a punch than I was expecting. So, will you tell me what you were celebrating or are you going to leave me to guess?"

She took one hand off the steering wheel to rest it on his thigh. "I think you can probably guess what we were talking about. Hell, I suppose you could have listened in with those enhanced senses of yours. She wanted to know how I was coping with your unexpected arrival. You know, since you're my soulmate and all."

"I was speaking with your father and brother at the time. Not to mention, it would have been rude to eavesdrop—wait. Say that last bit again." He couldn't have heard her correctly, but by God, he hoped she'd said what he thought she had.

"She asked me how I was dealing with the fact that I inadvertently bought my soulmate."

"But I thought—You said—Didn't you tell me she told you that you weren't destined for a true love of your own?"

Adina laughed. "I thought she had. I've spent years believing I was going to be alone. It turns out there was a minor miscommunication that day. She told me my true love was Stone. I thought she was being general, but she was talking about *you*."

"I told you I wasn't going anywhere," he said, barely controlling his urge to cheer. Adina was finally starting to believe in them and in what they could be.

"You're going to be insufferably smug about this, aren't you?" she asked, grinning at him.

"Utterly. But I promise I'll get over it in a decade or so. Fifty years, tops."

"In fifty years you'll still be exactly the same as you are now, won't you?" Adina's jaw tightened, and some of the light faded from her eyes as the reality of their situation dawned on her.

He covered her hand with his and squeezed it. "I don't know. Maybe I'll age normally now that I'm with you. Or maybe that's something that will change when your cousin gets me free from this spell. There are so many questions we won't know the answers to until Anneke is finished with her research. Until then, I'm going to try not to think about it too much."

"Does your patience and wisdom come with being older than dust or were you always this logical?"

"It came with age. And I am not older than dust, thank you. I'm in my prime."

"You're cheating. Magic stops you from aging. I bet you wouldn't be so damned sexy if you looked your age."

"Get us home, and I'll show you I'm still very much in my prime, brat. When six hundred years old you reach, look this good you will not."

She rolled her eyes and groaned. "Seriously? That's it. No more Yoda quotes. What did I do to the universe to get stuck with a *Star Wars* geek?"

"You must have been a very good girl. I'm a prize. I heard your mother say so." He loved teasing her like this. He loved making her laugh and basking in the warmth of her company. She was the sun rising after a night that he hadn't been sure would ever end.

"My mother thinks you're a—and I am quoting her directly here—hot hunk of manhood. I didn't even know those words were in her vocabulary!"

"Have I mentioned how much I like your mom?" he asked, snickering.

"If she ends up liking you more than me, I'm never going to forgive either of you."

He lifted her hand from his leg to press a kiss to her palm. "That could never happen. You're amazing. Not even I could hope to surpass you in her affections."

"Cocky old man," she grumbled at him as they pulled into her driveway.

The moment they neared the house, Stone felt the hair on the back of his neck rise in warning. Something wasn't right. He scanned the darkness beyond the car's headlights and finally spotted a black car parked in the inky shadows beneath the oak trees that grew in the front yard.

"When you park the car, don't get out. Lock the door behind me and stay in the car until I call for you."

"What? Why?"

"Someone's here and I don't get the sense they're friendly." He pointed to the other car even though it was unlikely she would be able to see it.

"You can sense their intentions? And what are you pointing to? I don't have your night vision, Stone."

"There's a car over there under the oak trees. I think they've been waiting for you to get home."

Adina pulled into her usual spot and shut the car off. "So there's someone lurking in the dark waiting for me to get home. Yeah, nothing nefarious about that. I'll stay here. You go work your badass, guardian mojo on them."

"I'm not sure whether to be flattered or insulted right now," he muttered and leaned in to give her a quick kiss on the cheek before getting out of the car.

"Be flattered, bad ass."

The moment his door closed he heard the locks engage. Satisfied she was secure for the moment, he headed over to the other vehicle. There was definitely someone sitting behind the wheel of what he could now see was a black SUV with tinted windows. Before he was halfway to the SUV, the driver's door opened and a bald man nearly as tall and wide as Stone stepped out. He made eye contact, nodded and then moved to the back door without a word.

Stone stopped walking and waited. Whatever was about to happen, a little space wouldn't hurt. He was almost disappointed when a slender man in his mid-fifties exited the vehicle and eyed Stone with suspicion.

"You're on private property. May I ask why you're here?" Stone asked.

"My name is Maxwell Webb. I'm here to discuss a business matter with Adina Diggersby. This is her home, yes?" the man asked as he flicked a non-existent piece of lint from the cuff of his perfectly tailored suit jacket. A faint scent of bergamot and cloves clung to the man, just strong enough to make Stone's nose twitch at the odd combination of odors.

Two sentences and Stone already didn't like this guy. "Do you often arrive at someone's private residence unannounced and uninvited to have business discussions this late in the evening?"

"I have come a very long way on a matter of some urgency. I believe that once I have spoken to Miss Diggersby, she will understand my somewhat unorthodox approach to meeting with her," Maxwell said, his gaze sliding past Stone to the vehicle he and Adina had arrived in.

"Tell me what you wish to speak to her about and I'll happily relay the message. It's up to her if she wishes to speak to you now or at a time more convenient to her." Two could play this game of painful politeness. This was familiar territory to Stone though admittedly it had been a great many years since he had an opportunity to play. In fact, there was something oddly old-fashioned about this fellow. His clothing was modern but tailored to echo another era. He was fastidious in dress and mannerisms and overly formal for this time. In fact, he reminded Stone of the men he'd known back before he'd been banned from his human form. Back before Pearl—God. Pearl's last name had been Webb, too. Surely that was a coincidence?

Maxwell's mouth pursed into a moue of distaste for a moment, but eventually, he nodded and began to speak. "Very well. I recently purchased an estate near Rochester, New York. The contract clearly stated that certain items were to remain in the house and on the grounds. The contract terms were violated when some of those items were sold without my permission. I am suing those responsible for this egregious error and of course, I am now left with the job of tracking down and reclaiming my legal property. Miss Diggersby recently took possession of a statue that rightfully belongs to me. I'm here to take it back, with recompense, of course. She'd know all this already if she'd answered my emails."

Stone kept his expression impassive, but his thoughts were racing behind the mask. "I see. You received no answer and decided the most reasonable action you could take was to drive out here in the dark, and wait for her to return. Forgive me for saying so, but I'm not a fan of your tactics, Mr. Webb. I will let her know what you wish to discuss. Stay here."

He turned on his heel and left Maxwell standing there spluttering at having been dismissed out of hand. The man was clearly used to getting his way. He was about to be sorely disappointed. Whether his story was true or not, Stone was bound to Adina now. He belonged here, with her.

He approached the car and gave Adina a quick smile and a thumbs-up gesture to let her know everything was alright. She got out of the car and started toward him, stopping when he held up his hand.

"What's going on? Who is that?" she asked the minute he was in earshot.

"His name is Maxwell Webb. He claims to have bought the Drummond Estate. At least, I assume that's the estate he bought since he also claims that some items were removed from the property before he took ownership. Somehow he's tracked you down as one of the buyers. He's here to get his statue back."

Adina's eyes narrowed. "A statue? The only statue I bought recently was you, Stone, and he can't fucking have you. You're mine!"

"You have no idea how sexy that sounds. I'm going to make you say it again and again once this guy leaves. He wants to talk to you, sweetling, but I told him that was up to you."

She squared her shoulders and nodded. "I'll talk to him. What I have to say won't take very long."

Stone winked at her. "Lead on, my lady."

Maxwell was still standing exactly where Stone had left him though his expression showed that he was entirely displeased by how things were going. "Miss Diggersby. Finally."

"My name is Diggersby, yes. I understand your

name is Maxwell Webb and you are here about a statue?" she asked, her arms folded across her chest.

"Yes. My statue. You have it, don't you? A gargoyle-type carving, about the size of a crouching man. An ugly thing, really."

"It's a very fine work of art, actually. If you think it's ugly, why are you bothering to retrieve it at all?" she demanded.

"I am not in the habit of letting my property be stolen, and that statue is my property. I am aware you didn't know that you were making an illegal purchase. In fact, I'm willing to offer you three times what you paid as a recompense for the statue's return."

"That won't be necessary, Mr. Webb. The statue belongs to me, and I will be keeping it," she said.

"But it's stolen!"

"I only have your word on that. Until you can prove to me that my purchase was illegal, we have nothing to discuss." Adina uncrossed her arms and pointed toward the road. "Good night."

Stone was having difficulty maintaining a straight face as he watched Adina go toe-to-toe with their officious visitor. He had no doubt that Maxwell would be back, but tonight Adina was the clear winner.

"This isn't over, young lady. You have something of mine, and I will see it returned to its rightful place. If you come to your senses, my phone number is on the back of my card. I will be in town for a few more days before returning home. I will be speaking with you soon, Miss Diggersby." He handed her a card which she took with reluctance.

"It's your time to waste. My answer is not going to change. Good night, Mr. Webb." She walked away from Maxwell without another word.

Stone took a single step toward Maxwell and glowered at him. "Be gone in five minutes and don't return here unless you've been invited. If I find you on this property again, I will consider you to be trespassing and act accordingly."

"There's no need for threats. I'm a businessman, not a thug," Maxwell said and gestured for his driver to return to the vehicle.

"You're a businessman who hires thugs. I'd say that's a very thin hair you're splitting. By the way, you now have four minutes and forty seconds." Stone didn't turn away until both men were in the vehicle with the doors closed. Once he heard the engine start, he joined Adina on the front porch where they both watched until the SUV's taillights vanished into the night.

"Well that was an unpleasant end to a nice night," Adina muttered as she leaned into his side.

"I don't know, I rather enjoyed it. That's the first time I've gotten to stare down an obnoxious bully in ages. Not to mention the pleasure I had in watching you take him down a few pegs. You're sexy when you're all riled up."

She scoffed. "You think I'm sexy first thing in the morning, too. No one is sexy when their hair is standing on end and they have sleep-lines crisscrossing their face."

"No one but you, sweetling," he said and wrapped a possessive arm around her shoulders before leaning down to kiss her.

It was a long time before she was free to speak again, but when she did her answer made him laugh. "Take me to bed, old man. I haven't forgotten your promise to prove to me that you're still in your prime."

In all his years of service, that was the best command anyone had ever given him. He scooped Adina into his arms and carried her, laughing, into the house. Tomorrow was soon enough to think about Maxwell Webb. Tonight was for celebrating the life he'd finally been allowed to live, and the woman fate had chosen to be his soulmate.

CHAPTER SEVEN

ADINA HADN'T BOTHERED to check her email until the morning after Maxwell's visit. Sure enough, there were two messages from him, both caught in her spam filter. She'd been too distracted by Stone's arrival in her life to worry about emails or anything else, which is how she'd missed them until now. Not that it changed anything. She had no intention of letting Stone go.

Over the next few days, they did their best to ignore Maxwell's attempts at contact. Fortunately, her phone was unlisted, so the only way he could harass her was by email. She heard from several of her friends that he'd been making inquiries about her in town, but Magic was too close-knit a community for him to make any progress that way. Anneke had offered to toss a vicious selection of minor spells his way, but Adina had declined. The man was annoying, but that was no reason to give him halitosis, gout, or hives. When she'd told Stone about Anneke's offer, he'd laughed, then muttered something about remembering to stay on her cousin's good side.

Three days later she and Stone were in town on a shopping run. They'd managed to deplete Adina's pantry and freezer since Stone's arrival. She needed to restock or they'd be trying to make meals out of condiments and pickles soon. Stone also wanted to pick up a few things, including clothes. Since they didn't know what would happen once Anneke found a way to undo the enchantments, he pointed out it might be wise to have a few articles of clothing on hand in case he lost the ability to conjure his own. Adina hoped that didn't happen. Having a lover who could get naked in two seconds flat had some definite advantages, not to mention the lack of laundry.

They were putting the last of their purchases in the back of her hatchback when her cell phone went off. The chorus of "Witchy Woman" started playing at full volume, startling Stone and making Adina laugh. "Anneke's calling. She probably came up with a new spell she wants to throw at Maxwell."

"That woman scares me. I'm glad she's on our side."

"You don't know the half of it," Adina answered before answering the phone. "Hey, Anneke, what's up?"

"I found it," Anneke said.

"Uh. Care to be a little more specific? What did you find?"

"I know how to free Stone. I found the spell they must have used to create him."

Anneke's voice cracked slightly and Adina's blood cooled at the sound. Whatever her cousin had found, it wasn't good. "Are you okay?"

"I will be. This is—I think it would be easier to explain this in person. Can you come by the shop? I'm here with mom right now. She helped me with the research."

"We'll be there in a few minutes, we're only a block or so away. See you soon." Adina ended the call and looked up to find Stone watching her intently.

"You look worried. Bad news?" he asked.

"Good news, I think. Anneke says she's found a way to free you. She's at her mother's shop just up the street. We can walk there in a few minutes."

Stone took her hand and started walking in the direction she'd indicated. "If it's good news, why are you frowning? Are you having second thoughts?"

"What? No! I want you to be free, Stone. That's not it at all. There was something in Anneke's voice, though. I got the sense this isn't going to be an easy fix and it worries me. I don't want to lose you. What if the spell goes wrong?"

Stone stopped in the middle of the sidewalk and pulled her into his arms. "It's not going to go wrong. This is going to work. I know it is. We're fated, remember? Your mother said so. You believed her when you thought she'd told you that you'd always be alone. Are you going to stop believing now that she's told you we're meant to be?"

"You're bringing my mom into this? Really? That's

totally unfair," she complained, but his words helped to ease her worries. If her mother had seen something terrible in their future, she wouldn't have been able to hide it, not completely.

"All's fair in love and war, sweetling. Didn't anyone ever mention that to you?"

"I've never been involved in either, so no, it hasn't come up."

Stone cupped her cheek and leaned down to kiss her as he uttered words she never expected to hear spoken to her.

"You're involved now, Adina Diggersby because as it happens, I'm falling in love with you."

She threw her arms around his neck and kissed him back. His mouth claimed hers in a scorching kiss that seared her soul and set her blood on fire with need. This was the man she wanted to spend her life with. She hadn't expected to find him. Hadn't believed he even existed. But he was here with her now and Adina couldn't imagine living the rest of her life without him.

"I love you, too," she whispered against his lips. "Does that mean we're both crazy?"

"Very likely. Especially since we're currently making a spectacle of ourselves in the middle of town," he said with a soft chuckle as he finally raised his head from hers.

She blushed as she looked around and realized they'd acquired something of an audience. Friends and neighbors were all looking on with smiles on their faces. Just when she thought it couldn't get any worse, someone started to clap and she buried her face against Stone's chest. "I'm going to die of embarrassment now."

"Not on my watch. I'm your guardian, remember? I'm here to protect you from threats of any kind, including death by mortification. Hang on to me, I'll get you out of here." He gathered her into his arms and lifted her without effort. Within seconds, she was being carried down the street and away from the now cheering crowd.

"My hero," she murmured as she eventually peeked her head up.

"I'm not sure I've earned that title. All I did was find an excuse to carry you around in public. I'm not even sure where I'm taking you. What's the name of this store we're going to?"

"The Sit-A-Spell Bookshop. You can't miss it, just look for the big, purple sign with a silver crescent moon."

"Got it. I'm going to guess that it isn't the run of the mill sort of bookstore."

"It is and it isn't. You'll see once we get inside. You can put me down now, Stone. Rescue complete."

"I don't want to. I like you right where you are." His arms tightened around her. "I'm glad you'll be with me when we hear what your cousin has learned."

"I am, too. You're not going to go through this alone. I'll be here, no matter what." She could sense he had something else to say, but she knew better than to push him. He'd talk when he was ready. None of this was easy for either of them.

"I know, sweetling." He pressed a kiss to her temple.

"So, about putting me down?" she reminded him.

"We'll get there faster this way."

She glowered up at him and poked a finger into the solid wall of his chest. "Was that a comment about my height, old man?"

"No. It was a comment about your adorable but very short legs."

"You're going to pay for that later," she teased, trying to keep the mood light despite what they were both feeling.

It worked, for a little while.

He stopped a few feet before they arrived at the store and set her back on her feet with care.

She took a step toward the door, then stopped when she realized he hadn't moved. "Stone?"

He smiled down at her, but there were shadows in his gray eyes. "I've been trying so hard not to think about it, but I can't do that any longer. It was easier to believe I'd never been a man than to know I had a life once and lost it. What kind of man was I? Did I agree to become what I am or was I forced into it? I have so many questions and I'm not sure I want to know the answers."

She took his hand in hers and squeezed it hard. "I can't imagine what this is like for you. I know you haven't wanted to talk about it. Not that there was much to talk about yet. We don't know anything except that you had a life once, and if Anneke is right, then you're soon going to have one again. You're going to be free, Stone, and I'm going to be with you every step of the way."

"And if I wasn't a good man? What if I was dangerous, Adina? What if I come out of this someone else? Someone who could hurt you?"

She shook her head. "They only took your memories, Stone, not your soul. You're the same person inside. I know it. Once we hear what Anneke has to say, we'll talk about it. Until we know what she's discovered, we're only borrowing trouble."

He tugged her up against him and wrapped his arms around her, holding her tight. "Thank you."

"You're welcome." She managed to get the words out despite being half-crushed against his chest.

Eventually, he released her, pressed a gentle kiss to the top of her head and reclaimed her hand with his. "Let's find out what your cousin has learned."

"One more thing before we go in there. While we're in the public areas of the store, everything's totally safe, but once we head into the back room try not to touch anything."

"Why not?" Stone asked.

"Because enchanted items don't always play well with other magical objects, and you, my love, are going to be the biggest magical thingy in there."

"Did you just call me a magical thingy?" he demanded, one dark brow arched in question.

"Consider it payback for the short legs crack you

made earlier," she said with a grin and headed for the front door of the shop. It was time for them to get some answers.

STONE WASN'T sure what to expect when he walked into the bookstore. It took his eyes a moment to adjust from the bright sunlight of the outdoors to the soothingly dim interior. When he could see again, he found himself surrounded by all manner of charms, wands, and other modern day magical accessories. Tarot cards, chalices, crystals, and rune stones shared space with a multitude of books. A woman that bore a striking resemblance to Adina's mother smiled in greeting and waved them toward her.

"Come in. Anneke said you'd be along shortly, but I didn't think she meant this soon. You must have been in the neighborhood already. Oh my, Adina. You did find yourself a looker, didn't you? And a big one at that. Hello, Stone. I'm Rayna, Anneke's mother. I've heard so much about you that I feel as if we've already met." She came around the counter and hugged Adina, then turned to Stone and did the same to him.

When she let him go, she turned to Adina and winked. "I think I'm jealous. All those muscles. Yummy."

"Aunt Rayna, behave yourself. You're a married woman. What would Uncle Nick say if he heard you talking like that?" Adina asked.

"If I'm lucky, he'd put me over his knee and spank me," Rayna replied with a wicked grin that made Adina groan.

"I don't want to know. I don't want details. We're going to go find Anneke now before you share anything else."

"A healthy sex life is a wonderful thing and nothing to be ashamed of!" Rayna called after them as Adina half dragged Stone toward the back of the shop and toward another door marked "Staff Only."

"Your aunt is…colorful," he said once they were out of earshot.

"That's a very nice way of putting it. At least now you see where Anneke comes by her quirks."

"Indeed. Are all the women in your family so forthright?"

"Oh yeah. Wait until our first family reunion. Seven generations of forthright and colorful in the same time and place. It's something else."

"Seven generations? How's that even possible?"

Adina glanced back over her shoulder. "Oh, right. I haven't mentioned the fact that some of my ancestors are still here, have I? Well, not here in town. They're in the graveyard for the most part. That place is more lively than the main street some days. Many of Magic's residents opted to stick around after they died."

"You're enjoying ambushing me with these little tidbits, aren't you? Every time I think I've gotten my head wrapped around this place, you throw in another surprising detail."

"Maybe. Can you blame me? You get the cutest look on your face when you're surprised, and everyone around here knows all of this stuff. You're the first person I've ever had to explain it to." She paused to open the door and then led him through.

Beyond the door was another world. The air hummed with energy and everywhere he looked there were books. Not the sort of books that had been for sale out front. These were old and well-worn. In fact, everything he saw looked to be ancient, from the books and scrolls to jars of unidentifiable powders and potions that lined one wall. Remembering Adina's warning, Stone kept his hands at his sides and moved with care so that he didn't touch anything.

"Anneke? Where are you? This place is a labyrinth, and I swear it gets more crowded every time I come back here."

Anneke called back. "I'm in the summoning and banishing section. Go past the jars of mandrake root, turn left at the scrying mirrors and you'll find me."

Adina snorted. "I bet that's a set of directions you never expected to hear in your life."

"Not so much, no," Stone muttered as he followed her through the maze. It wasn't long before they found Anneke. She was in a small annex leaning over a lectern that held a very large and clearly ancient tome.

"Sorry I didn't meet you at the door, I wanted to read over this one last time before you got here. I needed to be sure." She glanced up at them both and gave them a subdued smile.

"What did you need to be sure about?" Adina asked.

Anneke straightened up and pointed to the page she'd been reading. "My Middle English is rusty, so I had to double check a few things, but I'm certain now. This is the spell that created you, Stone. Now that I know what was done, I know how to undo it."

"At what cost?" Stone asked. He knew enough about magic, especially the kind his masters had used, to know that every act of spellcraft had a price.

Anneke sighed and ran a hand through her dust-streaked hair. "Do you want me to sugarcoat it or do you want it straight up?"

"Straight up, please," he said.

Adina made a small noise of dismay and leaned into his side, wrapping one arm around his waist.

"Let's start with the big one. If we do this, you won't be immortal anymore."

Stone wanted to cheer. "That's not bad news. That's fantastic. How long will I have?"

Anneke looked slightly surprised at his reaction. "That's another thing. I can't completely break the spell. If I undid it, I'd undo you in the process. So we found a work-around. I'm going to alter the spell so that your life is bound to Adina's. I mean, it could be anyone's, but I thought you'd want it to be her, seeing as how you're her destiny and all that."

"No!" Adina cried.

"No?" Her rejection hurt more than any pain Stone had ever experienced.

"No, I don't want you to die if I die. What if something happens to me? You deserve a long life, Stone. You've waited long enough to have it. This doesn't seem fair."

He turned to face Adina, cupping her face in his hands, so she had to look at him. "I would rather have one day with you than live a thousand empty years, sweetling. This is what I want. You are what I want."

"But..." she trailed off and raised her hand to cover his.

"I love you, and I want to spend the rest of my days with you. When your time here is over, I want to follow you into whatever adventures come next. You're not leaving me behind, Adina. Not ever."

"Wow. Where do I get me one like him, cousin? If you don't say yes right now I'm going to assume you've lost your damn mind."

Adina's lips quirked into a slight smile. "Then I guess I better say yes. I love you, too, Stone. I just hope you don't regret this someday."

"Never," he murmured and kissed her until Anneke had to clear her throat to remind them they weren't alone.

"So, that's a yes on the life binding thing. It means you'll age at the same rate Adina does. That's the only big physical change. You'll still be able to shift forms and use the other gifts the spell gives you. Flight, acute senses, and that nifty accelerated healing thing you can do."

Adina's brow furrowed. "What accelerated healing thing?"

He chuckled. "Surprise. Not fun when the shoe is on the other foot, is it? I can rapidly heal from any injury if I revert to my granite form for a few hours. It's how I get by without sleep or eating, too."

"And it's a good thing you heal fast. I fear you're going to need it," Anneke said, drawing his attention back to the matter at hand.

"More bad news?"

Anneke touched the pages of the book in front of her. "This is one of the nastiest spells I've ever come across. The last time you experienced it, they took your memory of what was done to you. This time…it's going to hurt, Stone. And when it's done, you're going to remember all of it."

"It'll be worth it to be free to live a real life," he said.

"And that leads me to the last bit of news. I can't be certain, but I suspect that when we rework the spell, you're going to remember who you were before this was done to you. In a sense, I'm going to finish what your first master started. I'm going to complete the merge between your two halves and make you one complete being. No more gaps or limitations. When it's done, you're going to be disoriented and probably have an epic hangover. I think it would be smart to assume that once the spell is cast, you're going to need some time in your granite form to recover."

"Is this dangerous, Anneke? If something goes

wrong, what could happen?" Adina asked, her voice heavy with worry.

"If I didn't think it was safe, I wouldn't do it. But you know that magic like this…it comes with a price. In this case, the price will be pain, both physical and emotional. There's no other way."

"When can you do it?" Stone asked.

"We've already been assembling the things I'll need. I could be ready by tomorrow night. I'd like to have my mother there, and your family too, if they're willing to come, Adina. They could lend me their energy, which would make this easier."

Adina nodded. "I'll ask them. I'm sure they'll want to be there. They know how important this is and how much Stone matters to me."

"I'd be honored to have them there," Stone murmured to Adina.

She looked up at him and smiled. "Of course they'll be there. You're family."

Her words hit him with all the force of a sledgehammer driving into his chest. Family. After centuries of being an outsider, he had a family and a woman who loved him. It was an incredible feeling. One he'd never expected to experience. "Thank you."

"You keep saying that, but I haven't done anything. Not really."

He gathered her into his arms. "What do you mean, you haven't done anything? You've saved me."

"Oh, well. Yeah. I guess I did, didn't I?" She was

smiling as she stood on her toes to meet his kiss. "In that case, you're very welcome."

Eventually, he let her go, and they made their way to the main store again. On the walk back to the car Stone found himself grinning, the light in his heart rivaling the glory of the sun overhead. He was going to be free. Adina would be the last master he ever had. He'd never have to live his life in the shadows again. He would be free to walk in the sunshine, and he planned on taking every step of his new life with Adina at his side.

CHAPTER EIGHT

ADINA'S STOMACH was doing backflips as she counted down the minutes until the ceremony started. They'd decided to use her studio for tonight's event, and so she and Stone had spent the afternoon clearing away her various projects and opening up the workspace. Stone had even taken the time to put away all her tools, which were now hanging in neat rows in their assigned spaces. It was the first time since she'd moved onto the property that everything was in its proper place.

Her parents and Hal were together, talking quietly amongst themselves while Anneke and her mother were going over the spell yet again. They muttered softly as they discussed pronunciation and pacing. The sound would almost be soothing if it weren't for the fact that Adina was too agitated for anything to calm her at the moment. The only thing that would make her feel better was getting this whole thing over with. Stone wasn't in any better shape. He was prowling the perimeter of the studio yet again. He hadn't stopped moving since they'd gotten out of bed this morning.

"Adina," he called her name and suddenly changed direction, coming straight across the floor to stand in front of her.

"Yes?"

"Before I do this. There's something I need to say."

He dropped to one knee, and her shock at his actions was only slightly lessened by her amusement that even kneeling, he was almost as tall as she was.

"What are you doing?" she asked, her heart hammering against her ribs.

"No way," Hal muttered. "I'm getting a gargoyle for a brother-in-law?"

"Not if you don't shut up and let him ask her first," Nadira hissed, elbowing her son in the side.

Stone grinned. "I think your brother figured it out before you did, sweetling. I've already spoken to your father, and he's given me his blessing. So, Adina Diggersby, would you do me the honor of marrying me?"

Adina tried to speak, but all she managed was a strangled squeak. When the words wouldn't come, she nodded in silent agreement.

"It's not official until you say it out loud," Hal called out, earning himself another well-aimed elbow from their mother.

"Halberd Elias Diggersby, you hush! I've waited a long time for this moment."

Adina finally managed to find her voice. "Yes. Yes, I'll marry you!"

"Thank you," Stone said and reached for her left hand. A moment later he pulled something from his shirt pocket, and she felt the slide of warm metal glide over her ring finger.

"When did—how did you manage to find a ring?" she asked as she lifted her hand to stare at the ring she now wore. It was a slender band of hammered silver, simple but beautiful nevertheless.

Hal snickered. "You're cute, sis, but you're not too bright—ow! Mom quit hitting me."

"Your father's skill isn't limited to weapons, sweetling. Once I asked his permission, he offered to make a ring for me to give you. Do you like it?"

"I think it's perfect," Adina said as tears welled up in her eyes.

Stone stood up and kissed her, and for once she didn't care who was watching. She threw her arms around him and held on tight. His mouth slanted over hers, claiming her with a fiery passion that left no doubt of his need for her. "I love you, and I'm never leaving you. Remember that."

"Damn right, you're not leaving me. We're going to be married." She kissed him and then burst out laughing. "Which means my last name is going to be Carver. How appropriate."

He laughed too, then kissed her one last time before letting her go.

"It's time," Anneke said.

For a moment, Adina was tempted to run back into his arms, but she knew she couldn't. This was his choice. His chance to have a real life and she wouldn't stand in his way no matter how afraid she was. His words from yesterday came back to her and she dashed away her tears and offered him a smile as she stepped backward, leaving him alone in the middle of the room. He'd told her he'd rather have one day with her than a thousand empty years.

"Come back to me," she whispered.

"Always," he said and then turned to face Anneke. "What do I do?"

"Kneel. Everyone else, join hands and come stand behind me," Anneke directed, her voice carrying more authority than Adina had ever heard from her.

Anneke placed several items into a blackened bowl, doused them in oil and set them on fire. As an acrid scent filled the air, she raised her hands and began to chant. Soon the air around them was crackling with energy. Adina stood between her parents, each of them holding tight to one of her hands as they lent their positive thoughts and support to Anneke. It could have been a few minutes or an hour that they stood together, but finally, something began to happen.

A nimbus of shadow gathered around Stone's body, deepening slowly until he was almost impossible to see. Energy danced and flickered inside the shadows. At first, they were only red and gold sparks, but the energy continued to build until it appeared as though Stone was caught in the center of a lightning storm. A crimson bolt flared, and for a second she could see him clearly, but then the bolt slammed into his chest, and he arched in pain.

She would have run to him, but her parents held fast to her hands, holding her back. A wind started to blow inside the studio, swirling and howling as the miniature storm raged all around Stone. She saw him struck by several more of the terrible bolts as Anneke's voice rose above the din. For a long, terrible time it was nothing but noise and light and fury, and then, suddenly, it stopped. The storm vanished, the wind died, and Anneke's final word echoed around the now silent space.

"It's done," Anneke said and nodded to Adina. "Go to him."

He was still on his knees, shoulders slumped, head bowed, and his hands on his thighs.

She raced to his side and dropped to her knees. "Stone?"

He lifted his head, and her heart ached as she spotted the blood flowing from his nose and the pallor of his skin.

"I know my name. My name…was William."

"William's a good name, but to me, you'll always be Stone. Are you okay? That was hard to watch." she said, stroking his cheek with a trembling hand.

He chuckled softly and took several slow breaths before speaking. "It wasn't much fun for me, either, but I'll be okay. Need to rest now. Tomorrow, I'll tell you about the man I was."

"I'd like that. I want to hear it all." She leaned in and kissed him, ignoring the blood that was smeared across his lips. "You came back to me, just like you promised."

He kissed her back. "Always."

She moved back with reluctance, not wanting to be parted from him but knowing he needed to heal. He shifted to his gargoyle form with a soft groan of pain and settled himself into the same pose he'd been in when she'd first seen him. Crouched low, with his clawed hands resting on his knees, and his wings folded over his back. The next change happened slowly and she watched, fascinated as the living being in front of her transformed into a cold and lifeless piece of sculpture.

"Stone's not the only one who needs some rest, ladybug. Why don't we walk you to the house and get you settled before we go?" her mother said.

"I'm not leaving him."

Her father came to stand beside her, his hand on her shoulder. "He'll be like this until morning. You can come back then and—

Adina cut off her father's suggestion with a negating wave of her hand. "No. I'm staying here. He's still aware, even like this. I want him to know he's not alone."

"Then I'm bringing you some blankets. You can rest on the couch and wait for him to wake up," her mother said.

"I should stay right here."

"Adina Diggersby, don't argue with your mother.

You can see him just fine from over there, and I'm not going until you agree to be sensible. You say he can see and hear you right now? So he knows you're planning on spending the night on the floor? What do you think he'd have to say about that if he were able to speak?"

Damn it. Her mom had a point.

"He wouldn't be happy," Adina conceded.

Nadira snorted with amusement. "Exactly. So, up you get. He's supposed to be resting, not spending his energy worrying about you while you worry about him."

"Yes, mom." Adina found herself obeying her mother though she did pause to kiss Stone's cheek before standing.

"You can stay here. We'll grab some blankets and bring them out. He's going to be fine, ladybug, and so are you." Her mom kissed her cheek, then herded her dad and brother toward the house. Anneke and her mother stayed behind to gather up their things and to say good night. Adina hugged them both, grateful beyond words for what Anneke had done.

Within ten minutes Adina was settled on her couch with enough pillows and blankets to be comfortable and still have enough left over to build a sizeable blanket fort. Her mother had even made her a mug of chamomile tea before she'd left. Curled up and comfortable, she lay quietly and watched the unmoving form of her fiancé. They hadn't even had time to celebrate their engagement yet. She was still coming to grips with the events of the day. So much had happened. Hell, the past week had been the strangest, most wonderful time of her life. It was like she'd fallen into a fairytale complete with a cursed hero, magic, and true love. The only thing missing was a villain. She snickered to herself. The only person she could think of that fit that description was the overly dapper and rather obnoxious Maxwell Webb. He hadn't even tried to call or email her today. He must have finally given up and gone home empty handed.

STONE WAS adrift in a place somewhere between wakefulness and true sleep when something intruded on his awareness. Someone was nearby, sneaking around Adina's home. He came awake in an instant and focused all his senses on the presence coming nearer. The crunch of a heavy foot on the gravel path came first. Then a faint cough muffled behind a hand. More than one person was out there, and none of them had good intentions.

With all his focus on the interlopers, it took Stone a moment to remember that he wasn't alone in the studio. Adina had stayed with him. He shed his granite form and rose to his feet, scanning the dimly lit interior until he spotted her. She was asleep on the couch, cocooned in blankets and unaware of the danger coming their way. He had to warn her. Moving silently, he crossed the studio and crouched down beside her sleeping form.

"Adina, wake up. We have company," he whispered.

She stirred almost instantly, her eyes flying open to stare at him with joy. "Stone?"

"I'm here. But we've got a problem. Someone's creeping around outside. I need you to get somewhere safe, sweetling."

"You woke me up to tell me to hide while you go kick some intruder's ass? Think again," she whispered back as her brow furrowed.

"My job is to protect you, remember? We don't have time for this discussion right now. Is there somewhere you can get out of sight at least?"

She still didn't look at all pleased, but she eventually nodded. "The loft. I'll head up to the loft, but boy, you're going to get yelled at later. You should have told me you were awake and feeling better."

He briefly considered telling her he'd only come to because of the threat outside and that he wasn't one hundred percent yet, but decided against it. She'd never leave him if she knew he was still feeling the effects of the magic that had torn through him a few hours ago. Anneke was right, it had hurt like hell, and he still needed time to assimilate the memories of who he'd been and what had been done to him.

The men outside weren't going to give him that time.

"Go. Stay out of sight. I'll be back once I've dealt with our uninvited guests."

She nodded and sat up. "I bet it's that idiot, Maxwell. I had hoped he'd given up. I guess not. I'll call the sheriff and let him know we've got trespassers."

"I suspect you're correct about it being our friend, Mr. Webb. I'll deal with them, and your sheriff can take them away." He stole a quick kiss before standing and helping her to her feet.

Adina headed for a ladder he'd never noticed before. It was mounted to the far wall and made of the same rough wood as the rest of the barn, making it hard to see. Perfect. She'd be safe up there.

The moment she reached the top of the ladder Stone headed for the door. There were two men roaming the gravel pathways between the studio and the house. He'd deal with them first. There was another man somewhere near the front of the house, and judging by the faint hint of bergamot and cloves in the air, that man was Maxwell Webb.

"Do you see the statue we're looking for?" One of the men whispered to the other one.

"I can't see a fucking thing, and all these hunks of rock look the same to me, anyway. Maybe it's in that barn?"

"Why would a chick keep a statue in a barn?"

"Why would any chick have this many statues, period? It's fucking creepy."

"Did you leave your balls in the car? Man up and keep looking."

"Fuck that. You already said you checked this place out the other day and couldn't find the thing. I bet it's in the barn. Why don't you check in with the boss man and I'll take a look-see."

"Just be quiet about it. The guy here last time was a big son of a bitch. If he's here, I'd like for him to sleep through our little visit."

"Now who needs to nut up. We can handle one guy and his little girlfriend. I'm checking out the barn, and then we can get the hell out of here."

"We go when he says we go. You know that."

Stone stepped into the shadows and waited. One set of footsteps retreated toward the house while the other set was coming his way. He'd take out the first one inside the barn where there was less chance of the scuffle being overheard. That way he could leave the studio knowing Adina was safe. The moment the door swung open. Stone was on him, clapping his hands over the stranger's ears to stun him before sending him flying into the nearest wall. There was a meaty thud as his head hit the timbers and then there was only silence.

Primed and ready for battle, Stone grunted in disappointment at the unconscious heap now sprawled on the floor at his feet. The man had gone down without even throwing a punch. If Webb was branching out into criminal endeavors, he was going to have to start hiring a better class of thug. He heaved the man over one shoulder and headed for the door. There was no way he was leaving anyone behind to threaten Adina. He'd secure this one and then go after the others.

Inspired by the two men's earlier conversation, Stone opted to tie his captive to the most vicious looking statue he could find. The garden hose he found to bind the thug with wouldn't hold the man for long, but it should keep him out of trouble long enough for the sheriff to arrive. Stone sighed as he checked the knot in the hose one last time. The sheriff's imminent arrival meant he was on a tight schedule. He had plans for Webb that required the two of them to have a few minutes of uninterrupted time alone. When he was done with him, Webb would never dream of bothering Adina again.

He took to the air to get a better look at where his remaining targets were. It only took a few seconds to spot them. Webb was a slender shape lurking near the oak trees where they'd had their first confrontation. The other man was headed back toward the studio. Stone recognized him as the driver who had been with Webb the other night. Big, heavy, and slow. Stone grinned as he dove down on the unsuspecting thug. Maybe this one would put up a fight. Despite his near silent descent his target sensed something and dropped into a fighting crouch mere seconds before Stone made contact. The two tumbled to the ground in a flurry of fists and cursing.

The fight only lasted a few minutes. It ended the moment his adversary caught sight of Stone's face and realized he wasn't fighting a man at all. His eyes widened and his mouth opened in a silent scream. Stone hit him with an uppercut before the scream could become real, and the man faded into unconsciousness still staring at Stone in horror.

"See you in your nightmares."

Stone was still securing the second thug beside his buddy when he heard voices raised in heated discussion near the front of the house. Angry words were being thrown back and forth, and one of the voices belonged to Adina.

What the hell was she doing out of the studio?

"I'm going to kill her myself," he muttered and started running to Adina. He shifted back to his human form along the way. He was more than capable of dealing with Webb in this form, and there would be fewer questions to answer later. When he came around the corner, he found his beloved standing between Webb and his vehicle, keeping the man at bay with three feet of sharpened steel. *She owns a sword?*

"…slimy, lying bastard. What part of no deal didn't you understand? You can't come onto another person's property and take things just because you want them. That's not how the world works!"

"I was merely attempting to repossess my property. I'll have you up on charges you crazy harridan! Threatening me with bodily harm. I'll sue!"

"No, you won't," Stone snarled.

"And who are you to tell me what I can and cannot do? The statue doesn't belong to either of you! It's mine. Everything the Drummond's had is mine, now. It's taken generations to right the wrongs done to my family and I need that statue to end this."

"You *are* Pearl Webb's descendant." Stone growled, the name leaving a bitter taste in his mouth.

"I—yes. How did you know?" Maxwell stammered, gawking at Stone in confusion.

"You're not the only one with an interest in the Drummond family history. You have the facts wrong, and I can assure you that the statue you seek does not belong to you."

"Of course it does. It's all mine."

Adina scoffed. "Not all of it. Trust me on that one."

"Why do you want it so badly, Webb?" Stone demanded.

"My grandfather made me promise to find it. It's a relic from a bygone era and my grandfather believed it was something special."

Adina raised her blade slightly. "It's very special. And you can't have it."

"I'll sue! You have no idea who you are dealing with, young lady!"

Stone grew impatient. There was only one way to end this. "No court of law can give you what you want. This is beyond the laws of men, Maxwell Webb." He shifted to his gargoyle form, unfurling his wings and roaring into the night sky.

"Beyond the—God! What the hell is that thing?" Webb squawked in terror and took several stumbling steps away from Stone only to be met with the point of Adina's blade.

"That's my fiancé. You were talking to him not five seconds ago," Adina said with a shrug.

"That's a monster! Get it away from me! What madness is this? Help! I'm being attacked!"

Stone curled his lip into a snarl, baring his fangs as he took a menacing step toward Webb. "Your grandfather was right about one thing. The statue you seek is special. *I* am the statue, and I am telling you that you will never own me. I belong to Adina, and that can never be changed. If you come back here again, I'll tear your limbs off while you watch and then strangle you with your own innards. I protect what's mine, little man. And she is *mine*."

Webb quailed in fear and started nodding his head so fast he looked like a possessed puppet jerking on a string. His mouth was open, but no coherent words emerged, only a babble of random sounds and frightened whimpers. He started to sway on his feet, and before Stone could say anything else, the man crumpled to the ground and curled into a ball, still babbling."

"Well, that was anti-climactic. I didn't even get to draw blood," Adina muttered.

"Why are you out here at all? And where in the name of all that's holy did you get a damned sword? I'm supposed to be the protector in this relationship, remember?

"You were busy dealing with the hired muscle and I didn't want this guy getting away. Once I called the sheriff, I went back to the house, grabbed Betsy here and went to have a chat with Mr. Webb. And hello, my dad and my brother are both bladesmiths. Did you forget that? I have several nice swords and a few daggers, too."

"Betsy? Your sword is called Betsy?" Stone ignored his aches and pains as he struggled to follow Adina's explanation.

"Bloodthirsty Betsy, actually. She was my twelfth birthday present." Adina hefted the blade and grinned. "Dad was horrified at the name, too."

A siren wailed in the distance, announcing the arrival of the local law.

"I can't believe he collapsed like that. I still had a few things I wanted to make clear to Webb. Do you think he can hear me right now?" Webb was gibbering to himself, so disconnected from what was going on around him that he might as well have been alone.

"I think you made a lasting impression. In fact, I think you may have broken his brain with that transformation. Normal people do not cope well with sudden revelations that monsters and magic are real."

"His family were always prone to hysterics. At least, the ones I knew. Delicate dispositions and an overdeveloped sense if importance."

"That sounds about right." Adina glanced toward the road. "You should probably revert to human form before Theo gets here. You do take a bit of getting used to."

Stone shifted to his human self, then walked over and took the sword from Adina's hand. "Later, we're going to have a little chat about what will happen to you if you go rogue on me again. Then you're going to show me these swords of yours. I think I'm going to want to borrow one."

She laughed. "I'll have Dad or Hal make you one of your own as a wedding present."

The siren's wail grew closer. "So, what are we telling the sheriff?"

Adina grinned wickedly. "The absolute truth. We'll just leave out the bit about you being a gargoyle. Trust me, Theo won't ask why the three of them are babbling about monsters. He knows better than that."

"There are definitely perks to living in a town like this one. What do you want to do about Webb?"

"Threaten to charge him with trespassing and anything else we can think of. Not that I think he needs any more incentive to stay away from me. If he ever regains his wits, I doubt he'll want to come back here. Whatever his grandfather wanted of him, he'll have to let it go."

"Good." Stone wrapped an arm around her waist and tucked her in against his side. "No one threatens what's mine."

"I love you, too," she said as the sheriff pulled in the driveway, bathing them both in the brilliant beams of his headlights.

Stone mustered a friendly smile and waited for the questions to start. It was going to be a long night.

CHAPTER NINE

IT WAS close to dawn by the time Adina closed and locked the front door and went to rejoin Stone in the kitchen. There had been statements to make, questions to answer, and no small amount of explaining to do, but it was finally over. Now, she had some questions of her own she wanted answered.

She found Stone rinsing out their mugs in the sink. Even with his back to her, she could see by the set of his shoulders that he was as tired as she was. With everything that had happened she hadn't been able to ask him how he was really doing. Now, she didn't have to. "I was going to ask how you're feeling, but I can see the answer for myself. You're not fully healed yet, are you?"

He set down the mug and turned to face her. "Not completely, no. That spell your cousin cast was as brutal as she warned me it would be."

"And yet you ordered me to go hide while you dealt with Webb and his men? You should have told me."

"If I hadn't been able to protect you, I would have flown us both out of there. I didn't need to be at my best to handle that bunch. I was in no danger. I was a soldier even before I was…whatever I am now."

She moved in close and hugged him. "You're Stone Carver. My fiancé and a badass gargoyle. Are you ready to tell me about who you used to be? Or do you need to rest more, first?"

"All I need is you, and maybe a few hours of sleep in that nice, soft bed of yours. You haven't been to bed yet, either."

"I didn't want to leave you alone last night."

"I heard what you said to your mom. I'm glad you stayed. It was comforting to know you were nearby. Of course, if you'd been in the house, maybe you'd have slept through our little adventure, so maybe it would have been better if you'd listened to your parents."

She laughed. "There you go, taking their side again. Is this going to be the way of things from now on?"

"I promise to only take their side when they're out of earshot. Do you want to sleep, or would you like to learn what I remember?"

"I want to know all of it, Stone. Watching you go through that was the hardest thing I've ever done. The only thing that made it bearable was knowing that when it was over, you'd finally be free. You are free, aren't you? I mean, do you feel any different?"

"I remember everything. And yes, I feel different. I cannot explain it, but something's changed. I believe your cousin was successful."

She laid a hand on his chest, over his heart. "Is my name still here?"

His shirt vanished beneath her fingers, revealing that the elegant script was still in place. "You'll be part of me forever, sweetling."

"Maybe I should get your name tattooed over my heart so we match. I guess that's my first question, too. Now that you know your real name, who do you want to be, Stone, or William?"

"You told me that I'd always be Stone to you and I agree. William Drummond died a very long time ago."

"Wait. What did you say your name was? But how —explain!" she said, stunned by what he'd just told her.

"My name was William Drummond, and I was my first master's bastard son. He gave me his name and recognized me when I came of age. He even saw to my education and training. I would have never inherited anything, but I was a member of his household and a man of means."

"So he did this to his own *son*? Why?" Adina demanded. She couldn't imagine how anyone would do that to their own child.

"I was out hawking with several of my half-brothers, and there was an accident. Simon, the youngest, grew bored and strayed from the rest of us. We didn't notice until we heard his horse screaming in distress. The boy had found a wasp nest and was prodding it with a stick. They swarmed, stinging the horse and sending into a panic. Simon was thrown and struck his head. He died the next day. Simon's mother blamed me for his death, and eventually, she turned them all against me. She'd always resented my presence and thought to have me turned out. Instead, my father did this to me as punishment. I'd failed to save one Drummond, and so he made me into this so I would be compelled to protect his descendants for all time."

"That's horrible! And then he took your memory so you'd never know any of this. Your father was a total bastard."

Stone chuckled. "I love that you are incensed over something that happened centuries ago."

"And I don't understand why you're not bellowing in a fury and breaking things right now. Granted, I'm grateful you're not busting up my furniture, but how are you so calm?"

"I'm not really calm. To be honest, I'm still trying to figure out what the hell I'm feeling. It's going to take me a while to work through it all. I lost so much, and then to have it all dumped back in my head at once after all this time..."

She hugged him hard. "So you might break things later?"

"Maybe. But I doubt it. I'd rather be building a life than tearing things apart. I've waited a long time to be free. Long enough to know when to let things go, and to cherish what I have in the here and now." He paused, then grinned down at her before reciting a familiar quotation. "Anger, fear, aggression, the dark side of the force are they. Once you start down the dark path, forever will it dominate your destiny."

"Really? You're going to quote Yoda again, now? What am I going to do with you, Stone?"

"I'm hoping you're going to take me to bed and let me make love to you before we both get some much-needed sleep."

"Quit quoting the short, green, swamp puppet, and you'll have a better chance of getting me into bed. Couldn't you at least quote Han Solo? *He* was hot!"

"God, I love you," he declared and kissed her.

Within seconds, her entire body was humming with pleasure. Her clit throbbed with sudden need and she rubbed her hardening nipples against the bare skin of his chest. His mouth claimed hers as his arms pulled her close and held her against the hard planes of his body.

She closed her eyes and kissed him back, letting go of everything else. There'd be time to talk later. Time to ask all her questions and help him come to terms with his past. They were going to have a lifetime together.

"Can I take you to bed now, or do you want to talk more?" he whispered between heated kisses, his hands already busy undoing the clasp of her jeans.

"No more talking. I'm all yours."

"You were mine from the moment you freed me, sweetling."

She nipped his lower lip. "As I recall it, I claimed you first."

"You did at that."

He cut off any chance for her to reply with a savage kiss, his tongue slipping past her lips to tangle with hers as he lifted her off her feet and carried her out of the kitchen. He covered the length of the house in seconds and set her down in the center of her bed before breaking their kiss to tear at her clothes with an eagerness that left her breathless and trembling with need.

It wasn't easy to undress while lying down but they managed. The moment her jeans were off Stone wished the rest of his clothes away. He wedged a knee between her thighs and covered her body with his as he kissed her again. The hairs on his chest rasped against her tender nipples, making her moan as the sensation sent sparks of desire shooting straight to her clit.

"Love me," she whispered.

"Always."

He began kissing his way down her body, nuzzling and nibbling a path to her aching breasts. His mouth closed over one tight nub and he sucked hard, drawing her deep into the scalding heat of his mouth. When she arched off the bed in silent encouragement, he took her other nipple between his fingers and began to tug and tease it until she was moaning with pleasure. His touch was rougher than usual, adding the faintest edge to his caresses that only increased her arousal.

Adina lifted her head to watch her lover at work.

His black hair fell around his face and the muscles in his arms stood out as he held himself suspended over her. He was the most amazing, beautiful, powerful man she'd ever seen, and he was all hers. She buried her fingers in his hair and tugged to gain his attention.

His low chuckle hummed against her breast before he lifted his head to meet her gaze. "Was that a request?"

"Please, Stone. I need you."

His gray eyes turned to molten steel and his lips turned up in a near-feral grin as he sat back so that he was kneeling between her legs. "Show me where you want me to be."

Blushing, Adina gestured to the apex of her thighs. "There."

"I said show me, Adina. Touch yourself where you want me to touch you and tell me what you want me to do."

Fresh cream flooded her pussy, drenching her already slick folds. Closing her eyes, she reached between her legs and parted her labia, pressing her index finger down on the swollen hood of her clit. "I want your mouth right here."

"Not until you open your pretty eyes."

Cheeks blazing hot now, she did as he instructed. Stone was watching her intently, his hard cock fisted in one hand as he waited for her to obey. Once her eyes were looking at him, he lowered himself so that his mouth was a scant inch from her pussy. That was when she realized he'd left the lights on. She'd never been so exposed before, and her first instinct was to clamp her legs shut and close her eyes again.

"You're beautiful, Adina. Don't you think about hiding from me," he said. Then his mouth was pressed to her tender flesh and his tongue was lapping at her clit. After that she stopped thinking about anything but his touch. His unshaved cheeks rasped along her inner thighs as he spread her lower lips and devoured her with long, slow licks that had her trembling beneath him. He groaned and licked her clit before sucking the delicate pearl into his mouth and biting down on it just enough to make her see stars.

He kept her on the knife's edge for what felt like an eternity, pushing her toward orgasm only to slow down before she could reach her climax. She was so close that she could barely draw breath to protest, but finally, she forced a single word out.

"Please," she begged and he gave her what she needed. Without warning he plunged a finger deep into her channel, curving it upward to stroke over her g-spot. She came on a broken cry, her hips bucking as her inner walls clenched and fluttered around his fingers.

She was still trembling with the aftershocks of her orgasm when Stone withdrew his hand and covered her body with his. They fit together easily, her legs framing his hips as he brushed several tender kisses to her mouth and cheeks.

"Mine," he whispered as his cock found her entrance and slid into her until they were one.

She laughed with joy as she twined her arms around his neck and responded using his own word. "Always."

They came together in a breathless blend of love and passion, losing themselves in each other until nothing existed outside the perfect bubble of pleasure that surrounded them both. Stone moved over her with relentless power, hips pumping as he claimed her with an intensity she'd never felt before. Hard and fast he rode her and she met each thrust eagerly, taking all he gave her and returning it in kind. She moaned his name time and again, urging him on as they raced toward the pinnacle together.

She came first, rising up on a wave of pleasure that crested and carried her away. She clung to Stone as he continued to make love to her, drawing out her climax until he finally reached his own. Her name was on his lips as his control snapped and he came with explosive force.

When they were both spent, she brushed a tender kiss to the corner of his mouth. He tasted of salt and it took her a moment to realize she was tasting her own tears. Her cheeks were wet with them, her happiness so complete that she'd been crying tears of joy.

"I love you so much," she murmured as he withdrew from her body and settled in beside her. He gathered her back into his arms and held her close.

"I love you, too. I think I loved you before we'd even met. You were my one light in the darkness and now you're the light of my life. You've given me everything I dreamed of and more."

His words triggered a fresh bout of tears, and she pressed her face to his chest so that her tears fell on her name where they were inscribed in his flesh. It was a permanent reminder that their lives were forever linked and they'd be together, always.

THE END

THE WORLD OF MAGIC, NEW MEXICO

Imagine...

A world where being abnormal is the norm.

Magic, New Mexico Kindle World brings together outstanding paranormal and science fiction authors to expand on the Magic, New Mexico series created by New York Times & USA Today Bestselling author, S.E. Smith.

It's time to fall in love with the action, adventure, suspense, and romance inside Magic, New Mexico. Curl up with each book now and discover what makes Magic, New Mexico different from the rest!

Curl Up with S.E. Smith's Magic, New Mexico series
https://www.magicnewmexico.com/books/

Susan lives out on the Canadian west coast surrounded by open water, dear family, and good friends. She's jumped out of perfectly good airplanes on purpose and accidentally swum with sharks on the Great Barrier Reef.

If the world ends, she plans to survive as the spunky, comedic sidekick to the heroes of the new world, because she's too damned short and out of shape to make it on her own for long.

You can find out more about Susan and her books here:
www.susanhayes.ca